I0596510

MIA KINGTIDE
GUARDIAN OF THE COAST

BY LUKE KILPATRICK

Copyright © 2025 Luke Kilpatrick

All rights reserved. No portion of this book may be reproduced in any form without permission from the copyright holder.

Book Cover by Luke Kilpatrick
Illustrations by Luke Kilpatrick

Third Paperback edition 2025

ISBN: 979-8-9924828-7-4

Pitter Patter Diving LLC

Luke Kilpatrick
luke@pitterpatterdiving.com
www.pitterpatterdiving.com

TABLE OF CONTENTS

To Diane, my amazing mother, and Teri, my incredible mother-in-law-to-be,

Thank you both for your dedication, thoughtful feedback, and encouragement as you proofed and beta-read this book. Your guidance means the world to me.

And to Mia, my wonderful daughter,
Your passion for the ocean and boundless imagination have inspired every moment of this story. This adventure is for you.

With all my love and gratitude,

- Luke Kilpatrick
February 2025

Chapter 1

A Cry for Help

The morning sun shimmered on the gentle waves as Mia Kingtide and her dad, Luke, paddled their green tandem kayak toward the sandy shore of Año Nuevo State Park. Behind them, *Pitter Patter*, their 26-foot cruiser, bobbed lightly on its anchor in a sheltered cove. The rugged coastline stretched out before them, dotted with windswept dunes and rocky outcroppings.

Mia leaned forward in her seat at the front of the kayak, gripping her paddle tightly. "This place is so beautiful," she said, her voice full of wonder. Luke, seated behind her, smiled as he steered them toward the shore. "It's one of my favorite spots," he said. "And I'll bet the elephant seals will be even more incredible up close."

The kayak glided smoothly through the water, the bright green hull contrasting against the deep blue waves. As they neared the beach, Mia could already hear the distant grunts and barks of the seals. It was a sound that carried a mix of power and mystery, drawing her curiosity even more.

Twelve-year-old Mia had always loved the ocean, it was impossible not to, growing up on the shores of Monterey Bay. Her life changed two years ago when she rescued an octopus being harassed by older kids while trapped in a tide pool. After Mia freed it, the octopus returned with an extraordinary gift: a magical shell.

The shell transformed Mia's connection to the ocean. It gave her the ability to communicate with most marine creatures, breathe underwater without scuba gear, and even move objects without touching them in certain situations. While she was still discovering the full extent of her powers and their meaning, one thing was clear: Mia was determined to use her gifts to protect the oceans and the creatures that call them home.

After pulling the kayak onto the sand and securing it with a rope tied to a log of driftwood, Mia and Luke began their walk toward the observation areas. The air was filled with the cries of seabirds and the rhythmic crashing of waves, creating the perfect soundtrack for their adventure.

As they followed the marked path through the dunes, Mia's eyes widened at the sight of the seals basking on the beach. The massive males, with their distinctive trunk-like noses, lay sprawled across the sand, while smaller females and juveniles rested nearby.

"Look at them," Mia whispered, her excitement bubbling over.

"They're amazing, aren't they?" Luke said, pulling out his camera to take a few photos.

But as they walked farther along the path, a faint, high-pitched cry reached Mia's ears. She stopped in her tracks, tilting her head to listen.

"Dad," she said, her brow furrowing. "Do you hear that?"

Luke paused, lowering his camera. "I hear it. Sounds like a pup… over there down that gully by the driftwood."

Mia quickened her pace, following the sound until she spotted the source—a small elephant seal pup huddled behind a large log of driftwood. Its gray, mottled skin was streaked with sand, and its dark, watery eyes were wide with fear.

The pup let out another faint cry, struggling weakly to move but collapsing back onto the sand.

"Oh no," Mia murmured, kneeling a few feet away. She could feel the pup's fear radiating like a wave.

"Hey there," she said softly, reaching out with her powers to communicate. "What's wrong?"

The pup's cries quieted as it turned its gaze toward her. "You… you can hear me?" it asked, its voice trembling with fear and exhaustion.

"Yes," Mia replied, keeping her voice calm and steady. "I can hear you. What happened?"

"I got separated from my mom," the pup said, its voice cracking. "The tide pulled me away, and I… I'm so tired. I don't know where to go."

Mia's heart clenched. She inched closer, her movements slow and careful. "It's okay," she said gently. "You're safe now. We're going to help you."

Luke crouched beside her; his face etched with concern. "What's it saying?"

Mia glanced at him. "It's scared and exhausted. It got separated from its mom and hasn't been able to rest or find food. It's dehydrated too." She pointed to the pup's dry, cracked skin.

Luke nodded grimly. "We'll call the Marine Mammal Center. This little one needs professional care."

The pup let out a weak whimper, trying to shuffle away but collapsing again. Mia moved closer, her voice soothing. "Don't move too much. Save your energy." She reached out her hand slowly, letting the pup sniff her fingers before gently stroking its fur. "You're really brave," she whispered.

The pup sniffled, its big eyes brimming with tears. "Will it hurt?"

"No," Mia said firmly. "The people at the center are going to help you feel better. I promise."

Luke asked Mia for her handheld VHF marine radio, then he set it to Channel 16 to call for help. He knew there was no cellphone service on this rural area of the coast. "This is *Pitter Patter* anchored off Año Nuevo," he said into the handset. "We've got an injured elephant seal pup on the beach—dehydrated, weak, and in need of medical attention. Requesting assistance from the Marine Mammal Center."

A crackling response came through. "*Pitter Patter*, this is the U.S. Coast Guard Sector San Francisco. We'll notify the Marine Mammal Center and send someone out. Stand by."

Mia stayed with the pup, stroking its fur gently

as it whimpered. "You're not alone," she said softly. "I'm right here."

The pup closed its eyes briefly, as if comforted by her presence. "Thank you," it whispered.

About an hour later, a white truck from the Marine Mammal Center pulled onto the beach. A woman with dark hair tied back in a ponytail climbed out, then got out a large animal crate from the back of the truck. She waved as she approached.

"Hi, I'm Carolina," she said warmly. "Thanks for calling this in."

Mia stood and gestured toward the pup. "It's really scared," she explained. "I've been talking to it to keep it calm, but it's really weak and hasn't had any food or water."

Carolina knelt beside the pup, her face full of compassion as she examined it. "You did a great job keeping it calm," she said. "This pup is definitely dehydrated, and it's showing signs of malnutrition. We need to get it back to the center as soon as possible for fluids and care."

She opened the crate and placed it gently on the sand, but the pup immediately started to panic.

"No! I don't want to go in there!" it cried, thrashing weakly.

Mia knelt down beside it, speaking softly. "It's okay," she said. "This crate will take you to people who can help, I promise."

The pup hesitated, its body trembling. "Will it hurt?"

"No," Mia reassured it. "It'll feel strange at first, but once you're at the center, they'll make sure you feel better."

The pup looked at her, its eyes wide with trust.

"Okay… if you'll visit me soon."

"Of course," Mia said, stroking its head gently.

With Carolina's help, Mia carefully guided the pup into the crate. The pup whimpered but stayed still, keeping its eyes on Mia the entire time. Once the door was secured, Carolina stood and nodded.

"Great job," Carolina said. "This little one's in good hands now. We'll take it back to the center, give it fluids, and monitor its health. If everything goes well, we'll release it back here in a few weeks."

Mia's face lit up. "Can I come visit it at the center?"

"Absolutely," Carolina said with a smile. "In fact, why don't you come for a tour? I'd love to show you what we do."

"I'd love that!" Mia said, her excitement bubbling over.

As the truck drove away, Mia stood with her dad, watching until it disappeared over the dunes. She turned to him, her heart full.

"That felt… amazing," she said.

Luke placed a hand on her shoulder. "You've got a gift, Mia. And you're using it to make a real difference."

Mia looked out at the sparkling waves. The ocean held so many challenges, but she was ready for all of them.

Chapter 2

Trawlers and Troubled Waters

The rugged coastline of Bolinas was barely in view as *Pitter Patter* cruised steadily northward, its red hull cutting cleanly through the calm waves. The foggy marine layer clung thick this morning, but Mia knew it would burn off by noon, revealing the small, eclectic town nestled between the ocean and the rolling hills of Marin County. Bolinas was famous for its rich marine life and off-the-grid charm, making it the perfect spot for their trip.

The Kingtides weren't here to fish. Instead, they had come to Bolinas to help document and monitor the health of the local kelp forests as part of a community science initiative. The area was a vital part of the coastal ecosystem, but invasive purple sea urchins and rising ocean temperatures had wreaked havoc on the kelp in recent years. A local environmental group had put out a call for volunteers to assist with the monitoring project, and Luke Kingtide had jumped at the chance to combine their love of adventure with a meaningful cause.

Mia sat on the side of the cockpit, her legs dangling as the salty breeze ruffled her hair. The thought of diving in new waters excited her, but it wasn't just the thrill of exploring. She was eager to learn more about how kelp forests supported marine life and how she might help protect them. Bolinas was home to vibrant underwater ecosystems, and the Kingtides were here to lend their skills to help ensure they stayed that way.

"Think we'll spot any sea otters?" Mia asked, glancing at her dad at the helm.

Luke grinned. "Maybe. I heard this stretch of coast has some of the best wildlife around. Keep your eyes peeled. You never know what you'll find here."

They were also planning to visit the Bolinas Lagoon, a haven for migratory birds and marine animals, and hoped to lend a hand with local habitat restoration efforts. For Mia, it was another chance to combine her unique gifts with her growing knowledge of ocean conservation and maybe make a difference in the process.

"This place feels so wild and untouched," Mia said, her excitement bubbling over. "I've heard the reefs here are amazing, like underwater jungles."

Her dad, Luke, nodded as he adjusted the throttle. "They are. Duxbury Reef and the deeper reefs beyond it are some of the most biodiverse spots on the California coast. Rockfish, sponges, hydrocoral, it's a hidden world under the waves. Just be ready. The currents around here can be tricky."

Mia grinned, zipping up her wetsuit halfway as she scanned the coastline. They had trailered *Pitter Patter* to Bolinas that morning and launched from the small ramp by the lagoon. Now they were heading toward the open water, eager to explore the famed reefs.

Luke eased back on the throttle, slowing the boat as they approached a sheltered section about 500ft off the one of the deeper reefs. "This is a good spot," he said. "You'll get a great look at the kelp forest, and I am marking a lot of fish activity on our sonar. Dropping anchor"

Mia grabbed her fins and mask, her waterproof GoPro strapped to her wrist. She double-checked the green waterproof bag, ensuring her magical shell and radio were secure.

"Ready to dive in?" Luke asked, keeping an eye on the water as he put on his scuba gear.

"Always," Mia replied as she back rolled off of the boat, her heart racing with anticipation.

The world beneath the surface was like falling into a dream. The kelp forest swayed gently in the current, its golden fronds reaching toward the sunlight streaming from above. Schools of shimmering sardines darted through the shadows, their movements as synchronized as a dance. The vibrant purples, pinks, and oranges of hydrocoral dotted the rocky reef, standing out like jewels amidst the greenery. Mia marveled at the intricate beauty of the underwater world, her movements fluid as she swam deeper.

But something felt off.

A shadow loomed in the distance, darker and more ominous than the rocky reef below. Mia swam closer, her stomach twisting as she realized what it was, a massive bottom trawling net, being pulled by a long cable. As she approached, the murky water near the reef came into sharper focus as it was being dragged across the seafloor.

Her heart sank. The net was tearing through the delicate reef, leaving destruction in its wake. Bright clusters of hydrocoral were snapped and shattered, their vibrant colors dulled as they floated lifelessly in the water. Among the wreckage, Mia could see endangered rockfish struggling to escape.

She swam back to her dad as he was descending the anchor line and signaled to him with a double thumbs up, telling him to head back to the surface immediately. They got back to the surface quick, Mia's breath coming in short bursts. "Dad!" she called out. "There's a bottom trawler fishing down there, right on the reef, it must have been hidden in the fog!"

Luke's expression darkened as he leaned over the side. "In a protected area? That's illegal."

"I saw the net dragging," Mia said, gripping the ladder to climb back aboard. "It's destroying everything. We must do something."

Luke nodded, his jaw tight. "We'll report it to Fish and Wildlife, but we need proof first. Bottom Trawling is highly regulated and this is way outside of the legal area for it."

Mia's eyes lit up with determination. "I'll get the evidence. If I can capture what's happening down there, they won't be able to deny it."

Luke hesitated, his protective instincts kicking in. "Be careful, Mia. Trawlers like that don't want to be caught. Stay out of sight and use the kelp forest for cover. Let's pull anchor and see if we can get a bit closer before you go back in. I have the trawler on radar so I know where it is"

Luke took *Pitter Patter* away from the trawler looking to get up current from it. He made a wide loop then cut the engine to drift near the other boat but keeping hidden in the fog. He dropped the anchor when he was in a good spot for the trawler to pass by but keep them hidden. "Ok Mia you can get in, but be careful!" Luke warned. Mia jumped off the back of *Pitter Patter* and into the ocean, making sure her VHF radio and GoPro were secure and working before she headed away.

As she swam toward the trawler, Mia heard a soft clicking sound. She paused, turning her head to scan the water. Two sleek shapes darted toward her, their gray bodies slicing through the blue-green depths.

"Are you Mia?" one of the harbor porpoises asked, its voice high-pitched and curious.

Mia's eyes widened in surprise. "Yes… How do you know me?"

The second grey and white porpoise circled her, its clicks and whistles excited. "We heard about you in Monterey Bay. The animals there said you can speak to us!"

"We've never met a human like you before," the first porpoise added, swimming closer. "What are you doing here?"

Mia smiled despite the urgency of the situation. "I'm trying to stop that trawler. It's destroying the reef and catching endangered rockfish."

The porpoises exchanged glances before nodding in unison. "We'll help. What do you need us to do?"

"Can you keep an eye on the trawler for me? Let me know if anyone comes close to spotting me."

The porpoises clicked in agreement, darting off toward the trawler. Mia swam behind them, her heart pounding as they neared the massive vessel.

The net was even worse up close. It dragged across the seafloor, tearing through the vibrant hydrocoral with ruthless efficiency. Rockfish and other marine creatures were tangled in the mesh, their desperate struggles futile against the heavy nylon.

Mia raised her GoPro, filming the destruction in vivid detail. She zoomed in on the broken hydrocoral, the torn kelp, and the flailing fish, capturing every heartbreaking moment. The trawler's name and home port were visible on the back of the transom, and she made sure to record those as well.

"They're taking everything," she whispered, her voice trembling with anger.

The porpoises returned, their movements agitated. "The crew's busy with the winch," one of them said. "They haven't noticed you yet, but be quick."

Mia nodded, focusing on her task. She swam closer to the net, careful to stay out of sight, and filmed the way it ripped through the fragile ecosystem. Her heart ached as she watched a large rockfish struggle against the mesh, its bright red scales dulling from exhaustion.

By the time Mia surfaced, her chest felt tight with emotion. The fog had cleared and she could see both boats, they were much closer together than she though, but the trawler was now heading away from *Pitter Patter*. "Dad!" she called, swimming toward the boat. "I got the footage."

Luke leaned over the side, helping her aboard. "Let's see it."

They reviewed the footage together, the weight of what they'd witnessed settling over them.

As Mia and Luke sat on *Pitter Patter*, the urgency of the situation pressed heavily on them. The trawler continued its destructive course over the reef, its massive net still dragging indiscriminately across the ocean floor.

"This can't wait," Luke said, picking up the VHF radio mounted near the helm. "We need to report this immediately. However, as soon as it goes over the radio they might try to get away."

Mia nodded, her wetsuit still dripping as she leaned against the side of the cockpit. "The longer they stay out there, the more damage they'll do."

Luke made sure the dial of the VHF radio was set to Channel 16, the emergency and calling frequency, and began speaking with practiced calm. "This is *Pitter Patter*, a 26-foot cruiser currently located near Duxbury Reef off the coast of Bolinas. We've identified a trawler illegally fishing in a no bottom trawl area, causing significant damage to the reef. Requesting immediate assistance from Fish and Wildlife and the Coast Guard. Over."

The radio crackled, followed by a firm voice. "*Pitter Patter*, this is the U.S. Coast Guard Sector San Francisco. Can you provide the name and home port of the vessel?"

Luke glanced at Mia, who quickly pulled up the footage on her GoPro and zoomed in on the trawler's hull. "The vessel is the *Hunter's Gaffe*, San Leandro, CA. Over."

"Copy that, *Pitter Patter*. Please maintain visual contact with the vessel but remain at a safe distance. We're dispatching a 47-foot response boat and a helicopter to your location. Fish and Wildlife will coordinate with us. ETA is approximately 25 minutes. Over."

Mia's heart raced as Luke confirmed their position and signed off. "They're coming, thank goodness the fog cleared" he said, squeezing her shoulder. "You did the right thing capturing that footage. It's going to make all the difference."

The sound of the helicopter reached them before they saw it, a deep thrum growing louder as the aircraft approached from the south. Mia shaded her eyes and spotted the bright orange-and-white MH-65 Dolphin helicopter cutting through the sky. Below it, a sleek 47-foot Coast Guard response boat powered through the waves, its crew standing ready on deck.

The helicopter circled above the trawler, its presence impossible to ignore. A booming voice came through a loudspeaker: "*Hunter's Gaffe*, this is the United States Coast Guard. Cut your engines and prepare to be boarded."

Mia watched intently as the trawler's crew scrambled on deck, clearly caught off guard, they must not have been monitoring channel 16 on their radio. The massive net was still dragging behind them, the destructive evidence trailing like a scar across the ocean floor.

The Coast Guard response boat pulled alongside the trawler with practiced precision. Armed officers in bright orange suits quickly boarded the vessel, their movements swift and authoritative. Mia and Luke listened as the radio crackled with updates from the Coast Guard.

"*Pitter Patter*, this is Coast Guard Sector San Francisco. The vessel is under investigation for illegal fishing in a marine protected area. We have secured the crew and are initiating an impound. Fish and Wildlife will be logging all evidence." Luke, replied with a quick acknowledgement to keep the channel clear.

A second boat arrived shortly after, this one bearing the insignia of the California Department of Fish and Wildlife. The officers onboard were marine biologists as well as law enforcement, equipped to handle the delicate task of documenting the damage and cataloging the illegal catch.

Through binoculars, Mia could see the Fish and Wildlife officers working methodically. They began hauling the trawler's net onto its deck, their faces grim as they uncovered the contents.

The radio crackled again, this time with a Fish and Wildlife officer's voice. "This is Officer Delgado with Fish and Wildlife. We are logging multiple endangered and protected species in the trawler's catch, including yelloweye rockfish, bocaccio rockfish, and hydrocoral fragments. These species are protected under California law and federal regulations due to severe population declines."

Mia felt a pang in her chest as she thought about the vibrant hydrocoral she had seen shattered on the reef and the rockfish that had struggled against the net. She knew how critical these species were to the ecosystem.

The radio continued to relay updates. "The captain and crew of the *Hunter's Gaffe* are being taken into custody for violations of the Marine Life Protection Act and the Magnuson-Stevens Fishery Conservation and Management Act," Officer Delgado reported. "The vessel is being impounded, the captain and boat owner Seward Fitchmann, and his crew have been arrested and detained, and the illegal catch will be documented as evidence."

Mia looked at her dad, her expression a mix of anger and relief. "They're going to pay for what they did, right?"

Luke nodded firmly. "They will. The evidence you gathered will make sure of that. And now Fish and Wildlife can use it to educate others about why these laws exist."

As the Coast Guard towed the *Hunters Gaffe* toward their station on Yerba Buena Island for further investigation, Luke turned *Pitter Patter* back toward the Bolinas lagoon. Mia sat quietly for a moment, the events of the day replaying in her mind. She thought about the devastation she had seen and the teamwork it had taken to bring the poachers to justice.

The two harbor porpoises surfaced near the boat, their sleek bodies cutting through the water as they swam alongside them.

"You did good today, Mia," one of them said, its voice bright and encouraging.

"Thank you," Mia replied softly.

"We all did." The other porpoise added, "Word will spread. More of us will know to look out for trawlers like that."

As they approached the harbor, the sun dipped

lower on the horizon, casting a warm glow over the water. Luke glanced at his daughter, pride shining in his eyes. "You know, not every twelve-year-old gets to say they helped save a reef and bring poachers to justice."

Mia smiled, her resolve stronger than ever. "It's not just about today, Dad. We have to keep fighting for the ocean. Every little bit helps."

Luke nodded. "And every time we do, we're making a difference."

As they got *Pitter Patter* ready to get back on its trailer, the porpoises disappeared into the deeper waters, their faint clicks fading into the distance. Mia watched them go, knowing she'd see them again.

Chapter 3

Sandy's Second Chance

"Pitter Patter, Let's get at'er," Luke said, tightening the last strap on the trailer as he echoed the phrase that had inspired the boat's name. Mia grinned at her dad, adjusting her green waterproof bag. "Ready when you are, Captain!"

As the truck pulled onto Highway 1, Mia watched the scenery shift from sandy beaches to rocky bluffs, the Pacific glinting in the distance. She couldn't stop thinking about the elephant seal pup she had helped rescue. Was it feeling better? Would it remember her? She clutched her notebook, where she had scrawled questions for the Marine Mammal Center staff.

The excitement built as the iconic Golden Gate Bridge, its massive towers reaching into the misty sky, came into view. Below, the bay sparkled with activity sailboats tacking against the wind, ferries cutting clean paths, and gulls wheeling in the salty breeze.

They towed *Pitter Patter* to the Sausalito waterfront and launched her at the Turney Street boat launch. Mia stayed aboard *Pitter Patter* while Luke took the truck back up the ramp and then stored the trailer in the parking lot. They then motored the cruiser up the bay to a guest berth at the Sausalito Yacht Club. The Kingtide's were long time members of the Monterey Peninsula Yacht Club and were happy to take advantage of their reciprocal arrangement.

"Do we get to keep *Pitter Patter* here in this beautiful spot for free?" Mia asked. "Yes, we pay our dues to be part of our club, but we provide the same thing for boats when they visit Monterey as well" explained Luke. "That's cool, I can't wait to go sailing with them again" Mia said. "We will soon, but first we need to keep your promise" Luke reminded Mia. The boat was ready for the next adventure, but Mia had to go visit a friend nearby first.

The Marine Mammal Center was nestled in the Marin Headlands, a stark contrast of rolling hills and dramatic coastal cliffs. Mia could hear the barking of the sea lions before she even stepped out of the truck.

Carolina, the cheerful staff member they'd met during the pup's rescue, greeted them at the entrance. "Welcome to the Marine Mammal Center!" she said, her ponytail swinging. "Ready to reunite with your elephant seal friend?"

"Definitely!" Mia said, her eyes lighting up.

Carolina led them through the main facility, where the sounds of marine life filled the air. Rows of enclosures stretched out, each housing a patient at various stages of recovery. Mia spotted a harbor seal basking on a rock platform, a sea lion darting through a rehabilitation pool, and a tiny otter curled in a corner of its enclosure.

"The pup's doing well," Carolina said as they approached a quieter area with shallow pools. Mia immediately recognized the little elephant seal. It had a wooden block with a number on it glued to his head. Though still thin, it looked stronger, its wide eyes more alert.

"Hi, there," Mia said softly, leaning over the edge.

The pup raised its head, blinking. Its voice, a gentle whisper in Mia's mind, came through clearly: *You came back.*

"Of course I did," Mia replied, her voice warm. "How are you feeling?"

The pup shifted, stretching one flipper. "They feed me fish, and it doesn't hurt to move anymore. But I miss the waves."

"You'll be back in the ocean soon," Mia assured it. "You're in the best hands here."

Luke watched from nearby, smiling as Mia chatted with the pup. He had grown used to her unique ability to communicate with marine animals, though it never ceased to amaze him.

Carolina gestured for them to follow her deeper into the facility, her voice animated as she explained the center's mission. "The Marine Mammal Center is one of the largest organizations of its kind in the world. We take in animals from the entire California coast, injured sea lions, stranded seals, even sea otters affected by oil spills. Our goal is always to rehabilitate them and return them to the wild, where they belong."

Mia hung on every word; her eyes wide as she took in the bustling facility. The air buzzed with activity: volunteers scrubbed down enclosures, veterinarians examined animals, and the distinct sound of barking sea lions echoed through the building.

"This place is incredible," Mia said, her voice filled with awe.

"It really is," Carolina replied with a smile. "We've treated over 24,000 marine mammals since we opened in 1975. Every animal here represents a chance to learn more about the challenges they face and how we can help."

Carolina led them to the outdoor rehabilitation pools, where several young sea lions darted playfully through the water. Their sleek bodies moved with effortless grace, their energy filling the air. One barked and splashed near the surface, sending droplets flying toward Mia. She laughed, wiping her face.

"They're almost ready for release," Carolina said, nodding toward the energetic group. "When they first come in, many are malnourished or too weak to swim properly. We monitor their weight, diet, and diving abilities every day to make sure they're strong enough to survive in the wild. Once they pass all our tests, we release them back into the ocean."

"How do you know where they go?" Mia asked.

"We tag them with small, harmless trackers," Carolina explained. "Some of the tags are temporary and fall off after a few months, but others transmit data for years. We can track their movements and see how they're doing in the wild. It helps us understand their behavior and survival rates."

Carolina pointed to a map on a nearby wall, dotted with pins and lines representing the travels of released animals. "See this one? That's a sea lion we released near Monterey Bay last year. It traveled all the way to Baja California and into the Sea of Cortez before settling near a colony there."

Mia's eyes sparkled with excitement. "That's amazing! So, you can actually see how they're doing after they leave here?"

"Exactly," Carolina said. "Every animal we track adds to our understanding of their species and their challenges. It's like solving a giant puzzle."

They stopped at an enclosure housing a harbor seal named Sandy. The pool was calm, the water rippling gently as Sandy swam in lazy loops. Her flipper was still bandaged, a stark white contrast against her sleek gray-and-spotted coat. Despite her injury, there was a quiet determination in the way she moved, her small body gliding smoothly through the water.

"That's Sandy," Carolina said, leaning against the railing. Her tone was warm, tinged with pride. "She was found tangled in a fishing line just north of Half Moon Bay. A group of kayakers spotted her struggling near a kelp bed and called our hotline. It's a good thing they did, she wouldn't have survived much longer on her own."

Mia knelt beside the pool, her eyes following Sandy's every movement. "How bad was it?" she asked softly.

Carolina's expression grew serious. "It was bad. The fishing line was wrapped tightly around her front flipper, cutting into the skin and muscle. By the time our team arrived, the wound was already infected, and she was severely underweight. Harbor seals are naturally solitary, so she didn't have a group to protect her or help her find food."

"Poor Sandy," Mia murmured, leaning closer. "That must've been terrifying for her."

Carolina nodded. "It was. But the kayakers stayed with her until our rescue team arrived. They kept their distance, but their presence probably kept predators away. Once we got her here, the first step was to carefully remove the fishing line. That took a while, it was embedded so deeply we had to be extra cautious not to cause more damage."

Mia's heart ached for the little seal. "What did you do next?" she asked.

"We cleaned the wound thoroughly and started her on antibiotics to fight the infection," Carolina explained. "The first few days were touch-and-go. She wasn't eating, and she was too weak to swim properly. But slowly, she started to improve. Now, look at her." Carolina gestured to the pool, where Sandy was practicing short dives, her movements still cautious but more confident than before.

Mia smiled, a flicker of hope lighting up her face. "She's amazing."

"She really is," Carolina said with a proud grin. "Harbor seals like Sandy are smaller and more delicate than elephant seals or sea lions, but they're incredibly resilient. They don't have a loud bark or roar like the others, they're quieter, more shy. But that doesn't mean they're any less fierce when it comes to surviving."

Mia watched as Sandy surfaced, her round, dark eyes scanning the enclosure. She let out a soft huff, droplets of water spraying from her nose. Mia leaned closer, her voice gentle. "Hi, Sandy. You're doing great."

Sandy paused, her gaze locking on Mia. Though the little seal didn't speak to Mia like the elephant pup, Mia felt a connection. There was something in the way Sandy tilted her head, as if she understood the encouragement.

"She's been practicing her dives every day," Carolina said, breaking the moment. "That's a key part of her recovery. Before we release her, we need to make sure she can hunt for herself. Harbor seals don't rely on groups like sea lions, they have to fend for themselves, so strength and independence are critical."

"How do you know when she's ready to go back?" Mia asked, her curiosity bubbling.

"We track a few things," Carolina explained. "Her weight is the biggest indicator. When she arrived, she was under 40 pounds, which is dangerously low for a harbor seal her age. She's up to 65 now, and our goal is around 80 before release. We also watch how well she dives, how much she eats, and how she reacts to her environment. If she shows signs of stress, we take it as a cue to slow things down."

Mia nodded, absorbing the information. "And then what? How do you release her?"

"We take her back to a safe location near where she was found," Carolina said. "For Sandy, that will be Ross' Cove near Half Moon Bay. It's away from heavy boat traffic, and the kelp beds there provide plenty of fish and protection. Before she goes, we'll tag her with a small tracker so we can monitor her progress. It's always a special moment to see them swim back into the wild." Mia's eyes lit up. "Can I come when you release her?"

Carolina smiled. "I don't see why not. It should be in a few days or weeks, she will let us know and I will call you to let you know when she's ready"

As they watched Sandy, Mia turned to Carolina with another question. "What's the biggest difference between harbor seals, elephant seals, and sea lions?"

Carolina grinned, clearly delighted by the question. "That's a great question. Let's start with harbor seals, like Sandy. They're the smallest of the three, usually weighing between 150 and 300 pounds as adults. They're also very quiet, they don't have a loud bark like sea lions. And they're not as social. You'll often see them resting alone on rocky beaches."

"What about sea lions?" Mia asked, glancing toward another enclosure where several sea lions were barking and splashing.

"Sea lions are much larger and more vocal," Carolina said. "They're incredibly social and live in large groups called colonies. They have external ear flaps and can 'walk' on land using their front flippers, which is something harbor seals can't do. They're also more agile in the water, great hunters and very playful."

"And elephant seals?" Mia prompted, thinking of the pup she'd helped rescue.

"Elephant seals are the giants," Carolina said, her eyes twinkling. "Males can weigh up to 5,000 pounds! They're famous for their large noses, which look like trunks. Unlike harbor seals and sea lions, they spend most of their lives at sea, diving to incredible depths to hunt for squid and fish. They're less social than sea lions but more so than harbor seals. And when males fight during mating season, watch out. It's a spectacle."

Mia giggled at the thought. "They're all so different, but they're all amazing."

Carolina nodded. "Exactly. Each species plays a unique role in the ecosystem. That's why it's so important to protect all of them."

As they prepared to move on, Sandy floated to the edge of the pool, her head bobbing just above the surface. Mia knelt down, her voice soft. "You're going to be okay, Sandy. You'll be back in the ocean soon, where you belong."

Sandy let out a gentle chuff, almost like a sigh of understanding. Mia smiled, feeling a surge of pride and hope for the little seal who had come so far.

"Come on," Carolina said, motioning toward the next enclosure. "There's more to see."

As they walked away, Mia glanced back one last time. Sandy had returned to her lazy loops in the pool, her movements more confident with each pass. It was a reminder of the resilience of nature, and the difference people could make when they chose to help.

In the medical lab, Carolina showed them where the most critical work happened. Shelves lined the walls, holding microscopes, sample containers, and medical equipment. A veterinarian and two assistants worked on a sea lion pup, gently cleaning a wound on its side.

"This is where we analyze blood samples, monitor infections, and develop treatment plans," Carolina explained. "We also study diseases that affect marine mammals, like domoic acid poisoning, which comes from harmful algal blooms. It's a big issue along the California coast."

"How do you figure out what's wrong with them?" Mia asked, peering at a set of X-rays displayed on a lightbox.

Carolina pointed to the images. "We use tools like these to check for broken bones or swallowed debris. We've found all kinds of things inside animals, fishing hooks, plastic bags, even rubber bands. That's why reducing ocean pollution is so important." Mia nodded, feeling a surge of determination.

As they walked back toward the enclosures, Carolina gestured to a group of volunteers cleaning an empty pool. "We couldn't do this without them," she said. "We have over 1,300 volunteers who help with everything, from feeding and cleaning to educational outreach. They're the heart of this place."

One volunteer, a middle-aged woman with red hair wearing a Marine Mammal Center Volunteer name tag reading Heather, smiled as they passed. "It's hard work," she said, pausing to adjust her gloves, "but seeing an animal swim back into the wild makes it all worth it."

Carolina added, "We also work with schools and communities to teach people about marine conservation. It's all connected, keeping the ocean healthy benefits not just these animals, but us too."

Carolina led them to a display highlighting the center's global efforts. "We also support conservation projects in other regions, like Hawaii. The Hawaiian monk seal is one of the most endangered seal species in the world. We've sent teams there to help with rescues and research."

Mia studied the photos of monk seals, their round faces and large eyes so similar to the animals she'd seen today. "I didn't know you worked in Hawaii too," she said.

"Marine conservation is a global effort," Carolina said. "The ocean connects all of us. By protecting one species, we're helping entire ecosystems."

As they returned to the elephant seal pup's enclosure, Mia crouched beside it. The pup looked more relaxed now, its small body stretched out on the deck.

"Do you think I'll be okay?" it asked quietly.

"You're already on your way," Mia said gently. "And one day, when you're big and strong, you'll be out there keeping the ocean in balance."

The pup let out a soft huff, its trust in Mia clear.

Carolina handed Mia a brochure as they prepared to leave. "We'd love for you to come back," she said. "We're always looking for volunteers. You'd be a natural."

Heading back down to Sausalito, Mia stared at the bay, her mind swirling with ideas. She thought about the dedicated staff and volunteers she'd met, the sea lions and seals healing under their care, and the importance of protecting creatures who couldn't speak for themselves.

Luke glanced over at her. "What's on your mind, Mia?"

Mia smiled, her green eyes sparkling with determination. "I'm thinking about how much more we can do. How every piece of trash we clean up, every animal we help, it all matters."

Chapter 4

Guardians of the Deep

The air in Sausalito was crisp as Mia Kingtide and her father, Luke, stood on the dock, looking up at the sleek figure of Vicky Vásquez. Vicky, founder of Rogue Shark Lab, exuded a calm, quiet passion for the ocean that immediately drew Mia in. She wore a navy-blue windbreaker embroidered with the Rogue Shark Lab logo and a friendly smile that reached her sea-weathered eyes. "Welcome to Sausalito, Mia," Vicky said, extending a hand to her. "Your dad's been telling me all about your adventures."

Mia shook her hand, grinning. "Nice to meet you! I've watched your videos about sharks. They're amazing and kind of scary."

Vicky chuckled. "Sharks get a bad reputation, but they're incredibly important to the health of the ocean. Without them, entire ecosystems fall out of balance." She crouched slightly to meet her gaze. "Did you know that over 100 million sharks are killed every year? Many of them just for their fins."

Mia's expression turned serious. "For shark fin soup, right? I read about that. It's banned in California, but doesn't it still happen in other places?"

Vicky nodded gravely. "Unfortunately, yes. Even though shark fin soup is illegal here, there's still a global market for it. And it's not just about soup. Bycatch, sharks accidentally caught in fishing nets, and habitat loss are big problems, too."

Luke, who had been listening quietly, chimed in. "That's part of why we're meeting today, Mia. Vicky's work includes protecting shark habitats, and she's going to show us some of the areas she's working to keep safe around the Farallon Islands."

Mia's eyes widened. "The Farallons? Aren't there great white sharks out there?"

Vicky smiled. "That's right. The Farallons are one of the most important feeding grounds for great whites. The islands are also home to a huge variety of marine life, seals, sea lions, even tufted puffins. It's one of the wildest places on this coast."

Mia glanced at her dad, her excitement growing. "Are we taking *Pitter Patter* out there?"

Luke grinned, handing her the dry bag with their day's gear. "You bet. Vicky's going to guide us, and you'll get a front-row seat to one of the most amazing ecosystems in the world."

Vicky glanced at the sleek red hull of *Pitter Patter*,

tied securely at the dock. "I've got to say, you've got a great little boat here. Perfect for navigating the Bay and beyond."

"She's not fast, but she's reliable," Luke said, patting the helm with affection. "Mia keeps saying we should paint an orca on the side to make her look tougher."

Vicky laughed. "Well, you'd certainly turn some heads."

Mia helped her dad load the last of their gear onto *Pitter Patter*, her mind buzzing with everything she'd just learned. She couldn't believe how much trouble sharks were in. Growing up on Monterey Bay, she had always thought of them as powerful and untouchable, apex predators at the top of the food chain. Now, she realized they needed help, too.

As Luke started the diesel engine, the familiar pitter patter of the diesel engine filled the air, steady and comforting. Mia took her spot in the cockpit, while Vicky stood beside Luke at the helm, pointing out landmarks as they cruised out of Sausalito.

The water shimmered under the midday sun, and the Golden Gate Bridge loomed ahead, its iconic orange towers rising like sentinels over the bay. Seagulls soared overhead, their cries blending with the hum of passing boats.

"There's something magical about going under the Golden Gate Bridge" Luke said, steering them toward the open ocean. "No matter how many times I do it, it always feels like the start of an adventure."

Vicky nodded in agreement. "It's the gateway to the Pacific, and to some of the most important marine habitats on the planet."

Mia leaned over the railing, letting the cool

ocean breeze whip through her hair. As they passed beneath the bridge, she felt a familiar sense of wonder, as though she were stepping into a world full of endless possibilities.

"Alright, Mia," Luke said with a wink. "Farallon Islands, here we come."

Vicky smiled, adjusting his cap against the sun. "Get ready, Mia. You're about to see the ocean in a whole new way."

And with that, *Pitter Patter* sailed into the vast, blue expanse, carrying them toward their next great adventure.

The waters beyond the Golden Gate Bridge were calm, though the faint haze on the horizon hinted at the vast Pacific's unpredictable nature. Mia sat in seat at the front of the cockpit of *Pitter Patter*, her GoPro ready to capture any marine life they might encounter. She kept her eyes peeled for the telltale splashes of dolphins or the glint of a sea lion's sleek body breaking the surface.

"Keep an eye out," Vicky called from the helm, his hand resting lightly on the wheel. "The Farallon waters are full of surprises."

Mia was about to respond when she saw it, a tall, black fin slicing through the water, followed by another smaller fin trailing close behind.

"Orcas!" Mia shouted, her voice brimming with excitement.

Luke immediately eased back on the throttle, letting the boat glide as the pod approached. "Good spot, Mia!" he said, grabbing his binoculars.

Within moments, the pod was upon them. The largest orca, a massive bull with a towering dorsal fin, surfaced just off the starboard side, sending a plume of mist into the air. Beside him swam a smaller female, her sleek black-and-white body shimmering in the sunlight. Two younger orcas followed; their movements playful as they darted between the adults.

Mia leaned over the railing, her heart racing. "Hello!" she called out, her voice carrying across the water.

The bull orca turned his massive head toward her, his intelligent eyes locking onto hers. "You're the human who talks to the sea," he said in a deep, resonant tone.

Mia nodded, a wide smile spreading across her face. "That's me. I'm Mia. Who are you?"

"I am Koro," the bull replied, his voice calm and commanding. "This is my pod."

The female swam closer, her voice softer but just as clear. "I'm Tala. We heard about you, little human. News of the girl who speaks to the ocean travels far."

Mia laughed, glancing back at her dad and Vicky, who were watching the encounter in stunned silence. "It's nice to meet you. Are you hunting today?"

The younger orcas swam in playful loops, their excitement bubbling over. "We've already eaten!" one of them piped up, his voice high and eager. "A fat ray and a shark!"

Mia's eyes widened. "A shark?"

Tala nodded, her tone matter-of-fact. "Sharks can be quite tasty, though they're not always easy to catch. We orcas are not afraid of them."

Koro chimed in, his voice rumbling with pride. "Fear is for those who do not understand their power. We respect sharks, but we know how to hunt them when necessary."

Vicky, overhearing part of the exchange, leaned closer to Luke. "Did she just say sharks to the Orca?"

Luke grinned. "Looks like Mia's getting another marine biology lesson. She has a special way of listening to the creatures of the ocean"

Mia turned back to the pod, her curiosity piqued. "Do you ever go near the Farallon Islands?"

Koro's eyes gleamed. "Yes, though we do not linger. The waters there are ruled by the great whites. They are cunning, but we are smarter."

Tala added, "Be cautious. The sharks are not your only concern. The great container ships pass these waters often. They do not see creatures like us, or you."

Mia felt a chill despite the sun's warmth. She had heard about the dangers of ship strikes to marine life. "Thank you for the warning," she said sincerely.

Koro dipped his head in acknowledgment. "You are brave, little human. And wise to listen. The ocean is vast, but it remembers those who treat it with care."

As if on cue, the younger orcas leapt from the water in unison, their bodies glistening as they arced through the air. Tala and Koro watched them fondly before turning back to Mia. Luke got some amazing photos of the stunning display.

"Travel safely," Tala said, her voice warm. "And remember, the ocean will guide you if you respect its ways." "Thank you," Mia said, her heart full. "I hope we meet again."

The pod began to swim away, their sleek bodies cutting through the water with effortless grace. Koro glanced back one last time, his deep voice carrying over the waves. "Watch the horizon, little human. It holds many secrets."

As the orcas disappeared into the open ocean, Mia sat back, her mind buzzing with wonder.

"That was incredible," Luke said, breaking the silence. "You've got some amazing friends out here, Mia." Vicky nodded; her expression thoughtful. "You've just had a conversation with one of the ocean's most intelligent predators. I don't think I'll ever forget that."

Mia smiled, looking out at the endless blue. "Neither will I." With that, Luke throttled up the engine, and *Pitter Patter* continued its journey toward the Farallon Islands, the lessons of the orcas fresh in Mia's mind.

The late afternoon sun gleamed against the glassy waves as *Pitter Patter* neared the Farallon Islands. Jagged cliffs loomed ahead, their rugged outlines stark against the endless horizon. The islands were shrouded in a ghostly mist that seemed to drift in and out of the sunlight, adding to their mystique.

Luke stood at the helm, his hands steady on the wheel as he navigated carefully between the islands. "Almost there," he said, glancing at Mia and Vicky. "Keep an eye out for the rocks near the surface. The waters can be tricky around here."

Vicky leaned forward, pointing to the island's cliffs. "These islands are some of the most important habitats in the Pacific. The Farallons are home to one of the largest colonies of seabirds in the world, common murres, auklets, and puffins nest here. And, of course, it's a critical hotspot for marine predators, including great white sharks."

Mia's eyes widened as she scanned the choppy waters. "Why are there so many sharks here?" she asked.

"The Farallons are part of the 'Red Triangle,'" Vicky explained. "It's a region from here to Bodega Bay and Monterey Bay that has one of the highest concentrations of white sharks in the world. The reason? Food. The area is rich with seals, sea lions, and other prey. These waters are teeming with life. Also, with us being about 25 miles off the coast, human activity has much less of an impact" Luke eased *Pitter Patter* into position, dropped the anchor and powered down the engine. The sound of seabirds filled the air, their calls echoing off the rocky cliffs. He tossed a glance at Mia, who was already slipping into her wetsuit. "You ready for this, Mia?" he asked with a mix of pride and concern.

"Always," Mia said, zipping up her suit. She double-checked the waterproof pouch strapped to her body, ensuring her handheld VHF radio and magical shell were secure. Her GoPro was mounted on her wrist, ready to capture footage for her marine life blog.

Vicky stepped closer; her tone serious. "Remember, Mia, these are apex predators. Respect their space and keep calm. Sharks can sense your emotions by feeling the vibration of your breathing and heartbeat, so confidence is key." Mia nodded. "Got it."

Luke put on his scuba gear, then helped Mia with her fins and weights. They slipped into the water, the cool Pacific immediately embracing them. As Mia adjusted her mask and fins, she felt the magical shell warm against her hip in it bag. It always seemed to respond to moments like these, as if readying her for the unexpected.

The underwater world unfolded before them. The kelp swayed gently in the current, its golden fronds creating a mesmerizing dance. Schools of fish darted around, their silvery scales catching the dappled light filtering through the surface. But it wasn't long before Mia sensed something larger in the water.

A shadow appeared in the distance, growing more defined as it glided closer. She squeezed her father's arm and let him know she was going to move a bit further away. Luke calmly hovered above the anchor, keeping an eye on Mia, ready if she needed his help.

Her breath caught as a great white shark emerged from the blue depths. The shark was massive, her body sleek and powerful, her movements fluid and deliberate. The dark eyes of the predator locked onto Mia, and for a moment, there was only silence.

Mia swallowed her nerves and spoke softly, her voice carrying clearly underwater thanks to the magic of the shell. "Hello. I'm Mia Kingtide. I mean you no harm."

The shark circled her slowly, her immense body cutting effortlessly through the water. "I know who you are," the shark said, her voice deep and steady. "The sea speaks of you, the human who listens."

Mia smiled, her initial fear fading. "I've been learning. There's so much to understand. What's your name?"

"I am Kallara," the shark replied, her tone both commanding and calm. "Why have you come to my waters, little human?"

"I wanted to learn more about you," Mia said. "You're one of the ocean's most important and feared predators"

The shark tilted her head, her movements graceful but deliberate, her large, dark eyes reflecting the filtered sunlight of the ocean above. Her voice, filled the water around them. "You, small human with the heart of the ocean, must listen closely. My kind are not the monsters your people paint us to be."

Mia nodded, the magical shell in her bag pulsing faintly, amplifying her connection with the great white. "I know, Kallara. I want to help change that."

Kallara circled slowly, her dorsal fin slicing through the water like a blade. "Then here is what I will teach you: Fear thrives in ignorance. Your kind fears what they do not understand. They see our teeth and strength, but not the balance we bring. We are the keepers of the seas, culling the sick and the weak, protecting the delicate balance of life beneath the waves."

Mia swam alongside Kallara, captivated. "How can I help them see that?"

The shark's movements stilled for a moment, as if considering. "Show them our world, as you see it now. Show them the mothers who travel thousands of miles to birth their young. Show them how we are hunted for our fins and left to die, and how that disrupts the ocean they claim to love. Tell them we do not seek them out; we hunt to survive, not to harm."

Mia's heart ached at Kallara's words. "I'll do more than tell them, I'll show them. I've been taking videos of the ocean, and I'll make one about sharks, about you. I'll explain how important you are and why we should protect you."

Kallara's massive form glided closer, her gaze intense. "Then I will share one more truth: The greatest danger in these waters is not us. It is the humans who fail to see what they destroy. The ships that pass above do not watch where they tread. Their engines drown out the calls of whales, their hulls leave trails of poison, and their nets… their nets do not distinguish between life and death."

Mia's chest tightened at the warning. "What can I do to stop them?"

"Warn them," Kallara said, her voice resolute. "Teach them. Speak louder than their fear, louder than their ignorance. The ships when slow do much less harm, have them keep the poisons to themselves and only net what they need, not more. And when you cannot speak, let your actions ripple across the currents. If one human listens, then another will follow."

Mia felt a surge of determination. "I will, Kallara. I'll do everything I can."

The shark tilted her head, a glimmer of approval in her deep eyes. "Then we have hope, little human. And with hope, perhaps balance can return."

As Kallara began to swim away, Mia called after her. "What should I tell people who fear you?"

Kallara's voice came as a whisper through the water. "Tell them to look beyond their fear and see what truly lies beneath. We are not monsters, we are guardians."

Mia watched the great white disappear into the blue, her heart pounding with purpose. She knew what she had to do. The ocean's story was hers to tell, and she would ensure that Kallara's truth reached the world above.

Back on *Pitter Patter*, Mia climbed aboard, her face flushed with excitement. Luke handed her a towel, his eyes scanning her expression. "What happened when the shark came so close to you?"

Mia smiled as she dried her face. "I met her. Kallara. She said sharks are fewer now, but they still protect the balance. She wanted us to know that the sharks are not monsters but guardians of the balance of the ocean."

Vicky leaned against the rail, her expression thoughtful. "It sounds like you've made another connection. These waters need voices like yours, Mia."

As the sun dipped lower in the sky, *Pitter Patter* turned back toward Sausalito. The ride was calm, the boat slicing through the waves as the Golden Gate Bridge came into view. Mia sat at the back of the cockpit, her mind racing with everything she had learned.

As *Pitter Patter* approached the Golden Gate Bridge, the rhythmic hum of the engine began to falter. At first, it was subtle, a slight change in pitch that might have gone unnoticed amid the steady crash of waves against the hull. But then, the engine sputtered audibly, causing Luke to glance at the controls with a furrowed brow.

"That's not good," he muttered, easing back on the throttle.

Mia, who had been seated at the bow, enjoying the cool breeze, turned to look at her dad. "What's wrong?"

"Not sure yet," Luke replied, his voice calm but serious. He adjusted a few knobs and gave the engine a gentle rev, but the sputtering grew worse, followed by a sudden loss of power. The boat slowed to a crawl; the once-steady purr replaced by unsettling silence.

Vicky, seated near the wheelhouse, leaned over. "Do you think it's the fuel line?"

"Maybe," Luke said, grabbing a flashlight from the console and heading below deck to inspect the engine. "Could be air in the line, or something clogging the intake. Either way, we're not going anywhere until I figure it out."

Mia bit her lip, glancing at the looming Golden Gate Bridge in the distance. They were so close to Sausalito, but with the current and the boat's lack of power, they might drift further out into the bay if the engine couldn't be restarted.

"Should we call for help?" she asked, her fingers instinctively brushing against the waterproof pouch where her magical shell was safely stored.

Luke's voice carried up from below. "Not yet. Let me take a closer look."

Mia sat near Vicky, the uneasy quiet of the stationary boat making her more anxious by the second. "What if we can't fix it?" she asked.

Vicky gave her a reassuring smile. "That's why the Coast Guard is here. If we need help, they'll make sure we get in safely."

A few minutes later, Luke reemerged, wiping his hands on a rag. His expression was grim. "Looks like we've got a blocked fuel filter. I can try to clear it, but it's not a quick fix."

Vicky nodded. "Let's call the Coast Guard. It's safer that way."

Luke grabbed the VHF radio from the console and tuned to Channel 16. "This is *Pitter Patter*, a 26-foot cruiser off the Golden Gate Bridge, experiencing engine trouble. Requesting assistance to reach Sausalito Harbor. Over."

There was a crackle of static, followed by a calm, authoritative voice. "*Pitter Patter*, this is U.S. Coast Guard San Francisco. We copy your request. What is your current position and status? Over."

Luke relayed their coordinates and situation, and the Coast Guard quickly responded. "*Pitter Patter*, standby. We are dispatching a 47-foot motor lifeboat to your location. ETA approximately 20 minutes. Maintain your position if possible. Over."

"Roger that. Standing by. Over," Luke replied, setting the radio down with a sigh of relief. "Help's on the way."

Mia exhaled, her shoulders relaxing slightly. "Thank goodness." Vicky gave her a reassuring pat on the back. "This is what the Coast Guard trains for. We'll be fine."

While they waited, Mia sat in the cockpit, watching the bridge grow larger as the current gently pushed them closer. The towering international orange structure was breathtaking, its massive cables silhouetted against the fading light of the setting sun. Despite her worry, she couldn't help but marvel at the beauty of their surroundings.

Before long, the distinct hum of a powerful engine reached their ears. Mia spotted the sleek 47-foot Coast Guard motor lifeboat cutting through the waves with precision. Its crew, clad in bright orange gear, moved with practiced efficiency as they approached.

"*Pitter Patter*, this is Coast Guard Motor Lifeboat 47212," came the voice over the radio. "We are approaching your location. Prepare to receive a tow line. Over."

Luke acknowledged the instructions and worked with Vicky to secure the bow cleats as the Coast Guard crew skillfully maneuvered alongside them. One of the Coast Guard members threw a line, which Luke caught and tied off.

The Coast Guard vessel's engine roared to life as it began towing *Pitter Patter* toward Sausalito. The steady pull of the towline was a welcome relief after the uncertainty of drifting. Mia watched the crew in awe, their teamwork seamless as they coordinated the operation.

As they neared Sausalito Harbor, the Coast Guard slowed, guiding *Pitter Patter* safely into a dock. Once secured, one of the crew members stepped aboard to speak with Luke.

"Glad we could get you in safely," she said, her voice kind but professional. "It's a good thing you called when you did. The currents out there can be unpredictable, especially near the shipping lanes." "Thank you," Luke said sincerely. "We appreciate your help."

The Coast Guard member smiled, tipping her hat. "Just doing our job. Take care of that fuel filter before you head out again." Luke nodded. "You bet."

As the Coast Guard vessel departed, leaving a soft wake in its path, Mia and Luke stood on the dock, watching the harbor lights twinkle against the darkening sky. The experience had been a reminder of the ocean's unpredictability and the importance of teamwork and preparation.

"Well," Luke said, resting a hand on Mia's shoulder. "That was an adventure." Mia grinned, her earlier nerves replaced with a sense of gratitude. "I'm glad we had help. And now we have another story to tell."

Vicky joined them, her hands in her pockets as she looked out at the calm harbor. "The ocean always has its challenges, but it also has its heroes. The Coast Guard definitely earned their title today."

Mia nodded, her mind already racing with everything she'd learned that day—about sharks, the islands, and the importance of protecting the ocean and those who relied on it.

As they walked toward a nearby diner for a well-earned dinner, Mia glanced back at *Pitter Patter*, her trusty red-and-white cruiser. Even with its hiccups, it had carried them through another unforgettable journey. And she couldn't wait to see where it would take them next.

Chapter 5

A Fresh Start at Ross' Cove

The early morning fog clung to the cliffs of Ross' Cove, the air cool and salty as Mia Kingtide stood on the sandy beach beside her dad, Luke. They watched as the small team from the Marine Mammal Center carefully maneuvered the crate holding Sandy, the harbor seal they'd helped rehabilitate. The seal's curious eyes peered through the grated door, her sleek, silvery-gray body shifting as if she could sense her freedom was near.

"Today's the day, Sandy," Mia said softly, crouching by the crate. Her voice was calm, reassuring. Over the past weeks, she had spoken to Sandy during their visits to the center, forging a connection that felt deeper than words. Sandy tilted her head, her large, dark eyes meeting Mia's. "Are you ready?" Mia asked gently.

Sandy let out a quiet, inquisitive chuff. Though not all animals responded to Mia's magical ability to communicate with words, she could feel the harbor seal's cautious excitement. It was a big moment, not just for Sandy, but for Mia too. She had been part of the seal's journey, from learning about her being tangled in a fishing line near Half Moon Bay to thriving under the care of the Marine Mammal Center. Now, she was helping to set her free.

Luke rested a hand on Mia's shoulder, his Mariners cap pulled low against the breeze. "You've done well by her, Mia" he said with a warm smile. "She's strong, and she's ready."

Mia nodded, her heart swelling with a mix of pride and nerves. "I just hope she knows how to stay safe."

Carolina, their friend from the Marine Mammal Center, approached with a clipboard in hand. Her ponytail whipped in the wind as she checked over the final release preparations. "Alright, team, it's time. Sandy's been cleared by the vets, and this cove is a perfect spot for her to reenter the wild. She's got plenty of fish to hunt and no immediate predators."

Mia glanced at the water, the gentle waves breaking over the rocky shore. A few harbor seals lounged on the nearby rocks, their rounded bodies blending with the boulders. It was as if they were waiting to welcome Sandy home.

Carolina knelt beside Mia, her voice soft but purposeful. "Would you like to do the honors, Mia? You've been such a big part of her recovery."

Mia's eyes widened, a surge of emotion catching her off guard. "Really? Are you sure?" Carolina smiled. "Absolutely."

Mia's hands trembled slightly as she reached for the latch on the crate. She took a deep breath, steadying herself, and then gently lifted the door. Sandy hesitated for only a moment before sliding out onto the sand. Her movements were graceful, her sleek body catching the morning light as she paused to take in her surroundings.

Mia stepped back, watching with a mix of awe and hope. "Go on, Sandy," she whispered. "This is your world."

Sandy chuffed once more, a sound that Mia felt was both a thank-you and a goodbye. Then, with a powerful push of her body, the seal made her way toward the water. The waves embraced her, and she disappeared beneath the surface with a splash.

"She's off," Luke said, his voice filled with quiet pride. For a moment, the small group stood in silence, watching the spot where Sandy had vanished. Then, to Mia's delight, Sandy surfaced a few yards out, her head bobbing above the waves. She looked again, this time more confidently, before diving down and swimming toward the nearby seals.

"She's home," Carolina said, her voice thick with emotion. "This is why we do what we do."

Mia felt a tear slide down her cheek, but it wasn't sadness it was pure joy. "Thank you, Carolina. For everything." As she gave her a big hug Carolina returned the hug and said, "No, thank you. It's people like you who make this work possible."

As they packed up the crate and gear, Luke turned to Mia. "What do you say we take *Pitter Patter* out for a little exploring?" Mia grinned. "I'd like that. I'm glad you were able to get her fixed up before we left Sausalito"

"A quick trip to West Marine, a new fuel filter and a bit of elbow grease was all it took, I am going to keep a few spares on board from now on," said Luke.

With Sandy safe and free, Mia and Luke headed back to the Harbor, where *Pitter Patter* waited patiently on its trailer. Little did Mia know, their next adventure was already beginning to unfold.

Chapter 6

Mavericks above and below

The sun broke through the morning fog as Mia Kingtide and her dad, Luke, prepared *Pitter Patter* for their latest adventure. The red-hulled cruiser bobbed gently at the dock in Pillar Point Harbor, its bright canvases vibrant against the muted gray of the harbor.

Mia zipped up her wetsuit, her excitement bubbling as she thought about their destination, Mavericks, the legendary surf break, just outside of the harbor on the north point of Half Moon Bay, was known for its massive waves and unique underwater topography.

As they got ready the noticed a group of crab fishermen at the docks, taking animatedly about the price of crab this year. They didn't look very happy, but they waved and smiled at Mia as they passed them to get on board.

"Alright, Miss Kingtide," Luke said, adjusting his Mariners cap. "You ready to see what makes Mavericks so special?" Mia grinned, securing her underwater camera in its waterproof housing. "Always."

As they motored out of the harbor, the salty breeze carried the distant calls of gulls and the low hum of the engine. The harbor's busy atmosphere faded into the serene expanse of the Pacific. Luke pointed toward the spot where Mavericks' immense waves would rise during storm season, but today, the water was calm perfect for diving.

Anchoring *Pitter Patter* near the reef, Luke double-checked his scuba gear while Mia adjusted her fins and mask. Unlike her dad, Mia didn't need a tank or regulator. Ever since the magical shell had transformed her life, she could breathe underwater as naturally as on land.

"You know the drill," Luke said, his voice steady as he slipped on his tank. "Stay where I can see you. No solo explorations, okay?"

"Got it, Dad," Mia replied, smiling. She loved diving with her father, and exploring Mavericks together felt like an adventure they'd always remember.

With a practiced motion, Luke fell backward into the water, his splash breaking the surface tension. Mia followed gracefully, the cool ocean enveloping her as the world above melted away.

The light swell moved them back and forth as they descended, shafts of sunlight filtering through the water to create a golden glow. The reef at Mavericks was a marvel of nature, sharp, jagged rocks rose like submerged cathedrals, their edges softened by layers of pink and orange anemones. Schools of silvery fish darted in unison, their movements synchronized like an underwater ballet.

Mia marveled at the geological formations that made Mavericks unique. Deep crevices carved into the reef funneled water in powerful currents, creating the conditions for the legendary waves above. She captured the scene with her camera, framing shots of the anemones and the shadowy caverns below.

Luke swam beside her, his movements slow and deliberate. He gestured toward a series of large boulders stacked precariously, their surfaces rough and etched with time. Using his flashlight, he illuminated a narrow passage between the rocks, revealing a tiny octopus tucked into a crevice.

Mia gave him an enthusiastic shaka, her face lighting up behind her mask. Scuba divers had adopted the shaka, a hand signal from Hawaiian surfers, a fist with the thumb and pinky sticking out and then wiggled back and forth. It communicates that what you saw was excellent, like a thumbs up on land. The thumbs up signal in Scuba diving means end the dive and go up to the surface, so divers use the shaka to replace its meaning.

Mia drifted closer to photograph the octopus with her GoPro, careful not to disturb it. The creature's skin pulsed with color, shifting from deep crimson to pale lavender as it studied her. Ever since she was given her magic shell, the connection to octopuses has been the strongest.

As they swam deeper, Luke pointed toward a section of the reef where the hydrocoral was particularly vibrant. The coral formed intricate patterns, its branches twisting and turning like an artist's sketch. Tiny shrimp darted between the branches, their translucent bodies catching the light.

Mia hovered near the rock reef, resting her hand lightly on the sand to keep steady. Her magical connection to the ocean always felt strongest when she was immersed in its beauty and today was no exception. She closed her eyes briefly, feeling the rhythm of the water around her.

When she opened her eyes, she noticed a small leopard shark gliding past. The shark's sleek body moved with effortless grace, and Mia felt a pang of sadness as she remembered what David had told her about the declining shark populations.

Her Dad signaled to her with his light, pointing toward a spot where the reef dropped off into a sheer wall. They swam toward it, the water growing darker as the sunlight faded. At the edge of the wall, a massive crack ran deep into the rock, its jagged edges lined with hydrocoral.

Mia positioned herself to capture the scene, her camera clicking as she took a series of photos. The images would be perfect for her marine life blog, where she shared the wonders of the ocean with her growing audience.

As she hovered near the wall, a sea lion appeared out of nowhere, twisting and turning in a playful display. It paused briefly to look at Mia, its large eyes full of curiosity, before darting away into the blue.

Luke tapped Mia on the shoulder and gave her the thumbs up signal towards the surface. His air supply was running low, Mia didn't need a tank, but they followed standard scuba buddy protocol even with Mia's special abilities. She nodded in understanding, signaled OK in acknowledgement and together they swam toward the anchor line to begin their ascent.

At 15 feet below the surface, they paused for the required safety stop, holding steady for three minutes to follow proper diving protocols to off gas any extra nitrogen in their systems.

Although Mia could breathe underwater thanks to her unique ability from the magic shell, she still adhered to standard decompression guidelines like any responsible scuba diver. Mia's grandpa had decompression sickness once from a dive trip in Roatan, and it was really scary, so they always did their best to follow every procedure to limit its possibility. Since neither she nor her dad knew how decompression might affect her physiology, they agreed to always follow recreational scuba diving safety protocols. Better to be cautious than risk the dangers of decompression sickness, even if Mia wasn't entirely sure it applied to her.

Back on *Pitter Patter*, Luke pulled off his mask, his face alight with excitement. "Did you see that wall? It's like nature designed it to create waves."

Mia nodded, scrolling through the photos on her camera. "It's incredible. The reef, the hydrocoral! It's like an underwater masterpiece."

As they secured their gear and prepared to head back to the harbor, Mia's thoughts drifted to the fishermen they'd passed that morning. She couldn't forget the frustration she'd seen on their faces, or the snippets of conversation about low crab prices.

"Dad," she said, breaking the silence, "do you think the ocean's challenges are connected? The declining shark populations, the fishermen struggling to make a living, it all feels related."

Luke sighed; his hands steady on the wheel as he guided the boat toward Half Moon Bay. "It is, Mia. The ocean is like one big web, every part is connected. When one-part struggles, the whole system feels it."

Mia stared out at the water, her mind racing. She didn't have all the answers yet, but she was determined to find them. There was so much to protect, so much to fight for. Today's dive had shown her the beauty of Mavericks, but it had also reminded her of the fragility of the world beneath the waves.

Chapter 7

A Price Too Low,
A Cost Too High

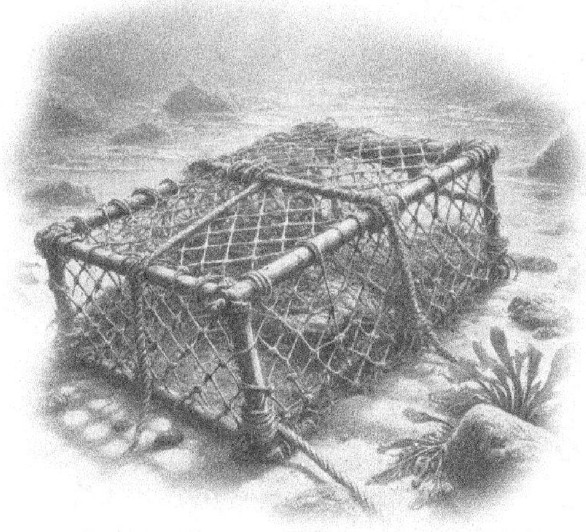

The salty breeze carried the faint scent of fish as Mia and Luke tied *Pitter Patter* to the dock in Half Moon Bay. The harbor bustled with activity: gulls circled overhead, fishing boats swayed in the tide, and crews hauled gear on and off vessels. Among them was an older man, his weathered hands coiling a thick rope as he leaned against a bright blue crab boat. His face was lined with years of hard work, his faded cap sporting the words *"Old Salt Fishing Co."*

"Afternoon," the man called, tipping his cap toward them. "New in town?"

"Just passing through, we are home ported just down the coast near Monterey Bay," Luke replied with a smile. "We're exploring up the coast, learning what makes each place special"

The man chuckled, his voice rich with the gruff warmth of experience. "Well, here in Half Moon Bay, it's the Dungeness crab. Best you'll ever eat, if I do say so myself. Name's Gus."

Mia stepped forward, intrigued. "Hi, I'm Mia. Are you a crab fisherman?"

"Been at it forty years," Gus said proudly. "The sea's been good to me, but I'll tell ya, it's not an easy life."

Gus leaned on the railing, his eyes scanning the harbor. "Tell you what. Why don't you and your dad come out with me tomorrow? I could use an extra set of hands. Might even teach you a thing or two about crabbing."

Luke glanced at Mia, who was practically bouncing with excitement. "We'd love to," he said, laughing at her enthusiasm. "What time?"

"Be here at five," Gus said with a grin. "And don't forget ya gloves. Crabs don't care if you're new, they'll pinch just the same."

As they chatted, Gus's smile faded, replaced by a furrowed brow. "Thing is, though, it's getting harder to make a living out here. Prices buyers are offering ain't worth the diesel to bring in a haul, let alone the new gear we're been pushed to use."

"New gear?" Mia asked.

"Ropeless traps" Gus explained, gesturing to a pile of sleek, modern-looking crab traps. "Cali's trying to protect the whales, which I'm all for. Entanglements a real problem. The state even gave us grants to help switch over. But these pots? They are a pricey lot. And when those buyers lowball us, it cuts deep. Can barely keep the boat afloat."

Mia frowned. "That's not fair. You're working so hard to do the right thing."

Gus nodded, his weathered hands gripping the rail, "Some of us are talking about a strike. If we stay in the harbor, maybe buyers will have to offer us fair prices. But it's risk. No fishing means no income, and for some folks, it's quick way for ya to lose everything."

The gravity of his words settled over them. Mia didn't know what to say, but her admiration for Gus and his fellow crabbers grew.

"Why do you call the crab traps 'pots'?" Mia asked.

Gus chuckled. "Well, the old ones were round, with ropes stretched between them, kind of like the pot you'd cook a crab in. Folks just started calling them that, and the name stuck."

"So, crab pots and crab traps are the same thing?" Mia clarified.

"Exactly," Gus said with a nod. "You got it. Alright, have a good night, see you tomorrow!"

The next morning after spending the night on *Pitter Patter*, Mia and Luke met Gus at the dock before dawn. The sky was painted in soft hues of pink and orange as they boarded Gus's boat, *Tide-to-Table*. Mia marveled at the simplicity and practicality of the vessel, its deck cluttered with traps, crab pulling cranes and bait buckets.

"Ya ready to work?" Gus asked with a wink. "Absolutely," Mia said, pulling on the gloves Gus handed her.

The morning aboard Gus's boat was a whirlwind of activity as they prepared to set the ropeless traps.

Gus, crouched on the deck, showing Mia and Luke the intricate workings of the ropeless system. The equipment gleamed with a mix of practicality and high-tech innovation, a modern solution to an age-old industry challenge.

"These pots," Gus began, tapping the sturdy metal trap with his knuckles, "are a game-changer. No more long ropes floating in the water, tangling up marine life or getting caught in boat props. Instead, they're sent down to the seafloor with a buoy or float that stays submerged until we call it up."

Mia leaned closer, fascinated as Gus held up a small, waterproof control device. "How do you get them back without the ropes?" she asked.

Gus grinned, clearly proud of the technology. "It's all about timing and sound. Each group of traps has a release mechanism attached to the buoy. When we're ready to retrieve it, this little gadget here sends an acoustic signal, a special type of sound to the trap."

He pressed a button on the controller, and a soft *ping* sound emitted from the device. "That signal tells the trap it's time to release the buoy. It pops up to the surface, and we haul the pot in just like the old days."

Mia's eyes widened. "So, the trap just waits down there until you call it? That's so cool!"

Gus nodded. "Exactly. And just so we don't lose a pot, ya must set it to launch the buoy after a specific time, this way if something happens or the sound signal doesn't work, in 2-3 days' time we can go get it. If that happ'ns we need to move fast after the release because we don't want anything to get tangled with it. The whole systems designed to protect marine life while still letting us do our jobs and not have to replace all of our pulling equipment."

He opened the trap to show the bait compartment, a small, enclosed space filled with chopped-up fish. "We load the bait here, drop the pot, and it sits on the bottom like a buffet table for the crabs. When it's time, the buoy floats up, and we pull it in."

Mia noticed a waterproof casing on the side of the trap with a bright orange casing. "What's that part for?"

"That's the timer, release and signal receiver," Gus explained. "The GPS receiver on the buoy sends out its location, so ya can always track where the trap is, even if it gets moved by a current or a storm, once its on the surface of course, it also says who's pot it is."

Luke examined the setup closely, clearly impressed. "It must've been a big investment to switch over to these," he said.

Gus nodded, his grin fading slightly. "It was. State gave us grants to help cover the costs, but even with that, it' wasn't cheap. The traps themselves cost more, and the tech needs maintenance. Still, it's worth it. We've already seen fewer whales and dolphins getting entangled, and the ocean's a little safer for everyone."

Mia ran her fingers over the smooth metal of the pot, thinking about how something as simple as a rope could cause so much damage to marine life. "Does every crabber use these now?"

"Not yet," Gus admitted. "State's pushing for it,

but some folks can't afford the upgrade, even with the grants. And others just don't like change. They think the old ways are good enough. But I'm telling ya, this is the future."

Once the traps were baited and prepped, Gus and Luke worked together to haul them edge of the boat. With a heavy *thunk*, the first trap splashed into the water, the trap sinking quickly out of sight. They moved along the edge of the underwater shelf, carefully spacing the traps to maximize their chances of a good haul.

As they worked, Gus shared stories of his years on the water. He recounted the thrill of hauling in pots overflowing with massive Dungeness crabs, the camaraderie among crabbers during a bountiful season, and the harrowing moments when storms threatened to capsize his boat. Mia listened intently, her mind swirling with images of the rugged life Gus described.

"You know," Gus said, leaning on the railing as they waited for the traps to do their work, "this job isn't just about the crabs. It's about respect, for the ocean, for the creatures we share it with, and for the people who came before us. These ropeless traps? They're part of that respect. A way to keep doing what we love, providing a good product, making a respectable living, and with causing less harm."

Mia looked out over the calm water, the horizon stretching endlessly before them. She thought about the technology Gus had shown her, the careful balance it struck between tradition and progress, and the importance of protecting the ocean for future generations.

As they waited for the crabs to find their way to traps, Mia couldn't help but feel a growing admiration for the crabbers like Gus, who were finding ways to adapt while staying true to their roots.

When it was time to retrieve the traps, Mia stood at the rail, her camera ready. Gus activated the retrieval system, and one by one, the buoys for the traps surfaced, ready to be raised by the crab pot puller. Each pot was a surprise, some brimming with lively crabs, others disappointingly sparse.

"Not a bad haul," Gus said, sorting the crabs by size and tossing back the smaller ones. "Only the legal ones come aboard. Sustainability's the name of the game."

Mia held a large Dungeness crab gingerly, its legs waving in the air. "It's beautiful," she said, admiring the intricate patterns on its shell.

"It's dinner," Gus joked, making her laugh. "But yeah, they're something special."

Luke helped load the catch into bins, his respect for the work evident. "This is tough. I can see why you're so frustrated with the low prices."

"It's not just me," Gus said, his tone serious. "A lot of us are barely scraping by. Something's gotta change."

By late afternoon, they returned to the dock, the air heavy with the smell of salt and fish. Mia helped Gus unload the bins, her muscles sore but her spirit energized.

As they stepped onto the pier, a group of crabbers gathered near one of the boats, their voices low but intense. Gus joined them, nodding at Mia and Luke to follow.

"We're meeting to talk about the strike," Gus explained. "Some want to go ahead, others are worried it'll do more harm than good. Feel free to listen in."

The group was a mix of ages and backgrounds, their faces etched with the strain of hard work. One man argued passionately for the strike, while another expressed concern about feeding his family during a shutdown.

Mia listened quietly, her heart heavy. She didn't have the answers, but she felt a deep respect for the crabbers' determination to protect their livelihood and the ocean they loved.

As the sun dipped below the horizon, casting the harbor in a golden glow, Mia turned to Gus. "Thank you for today. I learned so much."

Gus smiled, his eyes twinkling despite the weight of the conversation. "Ya welcome, kiddo. The ocean needs people like ya. Don't ever stop fighting for it."

The meeting of crabbers at the dock was tense, the air thick with worry and frustration. After hours of debate, they had finally voted to strike, agreeing to keep their boats tied up until the buyers raised their prices. It was a bold move, a desperate stand to protect their livelihoods and the weight of that decision hung heavily on everyone's shoulders.

As the sun dipped below the horizon, Mia and Luke walked back to *Pitter Patter*, their steps quiet in the fading light. The harbor was still the usual hum of activity, replaced by the silence of idle boats and the light splash of the waves along the break water.

Climbing aboard their cruiser, Luke turned on the cabin lights, illuminating the cozy space where they'd spent countless nights during their travels.

"Long day, huh, Miss Kingtide?" he said with a weary smile.

Mia nodded, slipping off her pink inflatable life jacket. "Yeah, but it feels like the right thing to do. I just hope everyone sticks to the plan."

Luke gave her shoulder a reassuring squeeze. "They know what's at stake. Get some rest, we've got another busy day tomorrow."

They settled into their v-berth, the gentle sway of the boat lulling them to sleep. Outside, the water lapped softly against the hull, and the distant cries of gulls faded into the night.

The next morning, the tranquility of the harbor was shattered. Mia woke to the muffled sound of raised voices drifting through the open porthole. She sat up, rubbing her eyes as the tension from the dock crept aboard *Pitter Patter*.

Luke was already up, sipping a cold sugar free Red Bull from the gally fridge. He glanced at Mia, his expression grim. "There's trouble."

"What's going on?" Mia asked, pulling on her jacket. The dock was alive with activity crabbers shouting, gesturing toward an empty slip where a crab boat was supposed to be.

"A rogue crabber," Luke explained, his voice low. "Looks like someone broke the strike. He went out before dawn to set traps, ignoring the vote."

Mia's heart sank. She could feel the frustration and anger rippling through the gathered fishermen. The fragile unity they had worked so hard to build was already starting to fray.

"Why would he do that?" Mia asked.

"Desperation, greed, maybe both," Luke replied, his tone heavy.

"Either way, it's going to make things even harder for everyone else."

The tension was palpable as they made their way to the dock, where the crabbers were gathered in heated discussion. Mia knew that today would bring more challenges than any of them had anticipated.

"Jesse's out there right now, dropping pots like nothing's happening," one crabber spat, slamming his fist on the dock railing.

"That's how we lose this fight," another said grimly. "If they think some of us will keep working, the buyers won't budge."

The air buzzed with frustration, but the situation escalated when Mike, a younger crabber with a sleek, fast boat, stormed down the dock. "If Jesse wants to break the strike, he can fish without traps. I'll cut every one of his floats," he growled, climbing into his boat.

Mia and Luke exchanged uneasy glances. "That's not going to help," Luke said, stepping forward. "You'll just create ghost traps that keep catching animals without anyone to harvest them. That's even worse for the ocean."

Mike glared at him. "What choice do we have? He's undermining all of us!" Mike brushed past Luke and headed down to his boat.

Mia tugged on her dad's sleeve, her eyes wide with urgency. "We can't let him do this, Dad. It's not just about Jesse it's about the ocean, too. We have to stop Mike."

Luke nodded, already moving toward *Pitter Patter*. "We can't stop him from cutting the lines, his boat is too fast, but maybe we can do something to stop the ghost traps. Let's go."

Before Mia could follow, Luke turned toward Gus, who was securing his own boat. "Gus, do you have a spare crab pot puller we can borrow? We need to retrieve those traps before they become a danger."

Gus frowned, glancing between them and the commotion on the water. "I've got an old one in the shed. It'll take some rigging to fit it on your boat, but if anyone can make it work, you can."

"Thanks, Gus," Luke said, already jogging toward the shed with Gus close behind.

While Luke worked with Gus to retrieve the puller and mount it onto *Pitter Patter*, Mia ran to the edge of the dock. She knelt, calling softly into the water. "Sandy? Are you out there? I need your help!"

The harbor waters were eerily still for a moment, but then a familiar face broke the surface. Sandy, the harbor seal they had helped rescue and release, bobbed up, her round eyes bright with recognition.

Sandy chuffed softly, tilting her head.

"I'm so glad to see you!" Mia said, relief flooding her voice. "There's a problem, some traps have been cut loose, and we need to stop them from becoming ghost traps. Can you and your friends help us?"

Sandy let out a short squeak of agreement, then disappeared beneath the water. Moments later, a small group of other harbor seals surfaced nearby, their curious faces peering up at Mia.

"She's got friends!" Mia called over her shoulder to Luke, who was busy fitting the puller to *Pitter Patter*'s cockpit gunwale with Gus.

Luke glanced up briefly, a faint smile tugging at his lips despite the urgency. "Looks like you've got your team. We'll need them."

Mia nodded, leaning closer to the seals. "Okay, here's the plan: follow us and help us locate the traps. Some of them might be too deep for us to reach, but I'm counting on you to help."

The seals chattered amongst themselves before Sandy gave an affirmative bark. They all disappeared again beneath the surface, leaving Mia feeling both hopeful and determined.

By the time she returned to *Pitter Patter*, Luke and Gus had finished attaching the crab pot puller. It wasn't a perfect fit, but it would do the job.

"Ready?" Luke asked, tightening the last bolt.

"Ready," Mia replied, her heart racing as she climbed aboard. Her focus shifted quickly to the task ahead saving the ocean from the ghost traps with the help of her father and their newfound harbor seal allies. Mia climbed aboard *Pitter Patter*, and Luke eased the boat into the harbor. The seals darted ahead, their movements quick and purposeful.

They left the harbor and headed out a few miles to sea, tracking the fast-moving blip on the radar that was Mike's boat. Another smaller signal appeared closer to the harbor. Jesse, the rogue crabber, heading back in.

Luke frowned as they watched Mike's boat veer erratically on the radar screen, each turn coinciding with the sinking of another float line. "He's cutting them all," Luke muttered, gripping the wheel. "We can't stop him; he's too fast."

Mia stared at the radar, her heart sinking. "Then we have to find Jesse before Mike ruins everything."

Luke grabbed the handheld VHF and switched to Channel 80A. "Jesse, this is Luke aboard *Pitter Patter*. Do you copy?"

There was a long pause before the radio crackled, and Jesse's voice came through, cautious and tight. "*Pitter Patter*, this is Jesse. What do you want, Luke?"

"We need to talk," Luke said, keeping his tone steady but urgent. "It's about your traps. Mike's out there cutting float lines."

"What?" Jesse's voice cracked over the radio. "Cutting them? All of them?"

"He said he was going to do it, and we see him on radar," Luke confirmed. "He's fast, Jesse. We can't stop him, but we can help you get your gear back. We need the coordinates for your traps."

There was another long pause, filled only with the hum of the VHF static. Then Jesse's voice came back, shaking with anger and despair. "You don't get it. I just repowered my boat to an electric engine with batteries. It cost me everything I had, but it's what the buyers want sustainability this, eco-friendly that, I wanted to be the first crabs brought to market without oil. If I lose my traps, I lose the boat. And that boat's been in my family for three generations."

Mia leaned forward, her voice calm and steady. "Jesse, we understand how much your boat and traps mean to you. But if Mike cuts all your lines, your gear will become ghost traps, and it'll hurt the ocean and everyone else who fishes here. Let us help you. If we have the coordinates, we can recover the traps."

Jesse didn't respond immediately. The silence felt heavy, like the weight of his decision was pressing down on him. "Jesse, please," Mia added, her tone soft but firm. "We can't undo what's already happened, but we can stop it from getting worse. Let us save what we can."

There was a long sigh over the radio, and then Jesse replied. "Alright. I'll send you the coordinates. I just upgraded to Wi-Fi on the chartplotter, so I can transfer them to you."

Luke quickly grabbed his tablet, already linked to the Simrad chartplotter on *Pitter Patter*. "We're ready to receive," he said.

Moments later, the screen on the chartplotter blinked as the data transfer began. Little icons began appearing on their navigation map, marking the locations of Jesse's traps.

"Got it," Luke said, checking the chartplotter. "Thanks, Jesse. We'll get to work right away."

"Good luck, I am going to come to you and stay close by, if I come back in with empty traps, maybe they will go easy on me for breaking the strike" Jesse said, his voice barely audible before the radio went silent.

Luke studied the screen, plotting the most efficient route to cover all the traps. "Let's move," he said, pushing the throttle forward. "We've got work to do."

Mia nodded, her resolve firm. They couldn't stop Mike from causing harm, but they wouldn't let those traps remain as ghost gear. Not today.

When they got to the first location, the seals were waiting for them. Mia checked her gear, tightening her mask and slipping the magical shell into her wetsuit pocket. "I can't go deeper than eighty feet, but the seals can," she said. "Let's work together."

The process was exhausting. Some of Jesse's traps were over 300 feet deep on the seafloor, requiring careful coordination between Mia, the seals, and Luke aboard *Pitter Patter*. Using the borrowed pot puller and the seals' incredible diving skills, they managed to locate each sunken trap. One by one, the traps emerged from the depths.

Mia worked tirelessly, taking the line to the surface to be threaded into the puller, while the seals dove deep for the next one. Each trap was emptied of crabs, and some of the bait holders were gone, but the sturdy frames were still repairable.

As they hoisted the last trap onto the deck, Mia wiped her forehead and climbed up the ladder onto the back of *Pitter Patter*. "That's the last one," she said, slumping onto a bench.

Luke gave her a proud smile as he secured the trap. "We couldn't have done it without you or your friends."

The seals popped their heads above the water, chattering happily on of the older seals called out. "You're welcome, Mia! Call us anytime."

Mia leaned over the side, addressing Sandy directly. "Thank you for going so deep. You were amazing."

Sandy gave a playful squeak and disappeared under the waves with the others.

The sun was beginning to dip toward the horizon as Luke maneuvered *Pitter Patter* to a spot just outside the usual crabbing areas, a location Jesse had chosen carefully to avoid suspicion. The traps were loaded onto Jesse's boat one by one. Each empty but intact trap was a small victory.

"These traps are all still repairable," Luke said as he helped secure the last one. "You'll need to fix them up, but they can be upgraded to ropeless."

Jesse stood silently for a moment, his hands

gripping the rail of his boat as he stared at the traps. "I don't know how to thank you," he said, his voice thick with emotion. "If I'd lost these… I'd have nothing left."

Mia leaned against the railing of *Pitter Patter*, her arms sore but her heart full. "We couldn't just leave them out there. Ghost traps hurt the ocean, and they would have hurt you, too."

Jesse gave a short, shaky laugh. "I don't deserve this kindness, not after breaking the strike."

"You made a mistake," Luke said firmly, "but what matters is what you do next. Start fresh. Work with the others to make things better for everyone, for the crabbers and the ocean."

Jesse nodded slowly, his expression a mix of gratitude and determination. "I will. I'll upgrade these traps to ropeless, and I'll work with the other guys to figure out a better way forward."

Mia reached out and touched one of the traps, her voice soft but steady. "You'll also have to tell them the truth eventually. About what happened, and how you're trying to fix things. That's how you earn back trust."

Jesse nodded again, his jaw tightening. "You're right. I'll face whatever comes."

As they parted ways, *Pitter Patter* turned back toward the harbor while Jesse headed in a different direction, timing his return to avoid too many questions.

Back at the dock, the mood was tense as word spread about what had happened. The rogue crabber, Jesse, returned to find the other crabbers angry and waiting. Mike, too, faced a harsh reception for his reckless actions.

The crabbers called an emergency meeting. After hours of debate, they reached a decision: Jesse would have to pay a portion of his profits into the strike fund to support the families struggling during the shutdown and when the season gets delayed. Mike, meanwhile, was ordered to cover the cost of upgrading Jesse's traps to ropeless ones, ensuring no more ghost traps would harm the ocean.

"It's about accountability," one crabber said. "We can't let one bad decision ruin what we're all fighting for."

The strike continued for three more days. On the fourth morning, the buyers finally caved, offering double the original price. Cheers erupted on the dock as the crabbers celebrated their victory.

As the sun set over Half Moon Bay, Mia sat on *Pitter Patter*'s deck, watching the harbor lights twinkle on the water. Luke joined her, handing her a mug of hot cocoa.

"That was intense," he said. "But I'm proud of how you handled it."

Mia nodded, her thoughts swirling. "It's amazing how much these crabbers care not just about their livelihood, but about the ocean. I wish more people understood that."

"They will," Luke said. "Especially if people like you keep telling their stories."

Mia smiled, sipping her cocoa as the harbor seals splashed softly in the distance. The fight for fairness and conservation wasn't over, but for tonight, she was content to savor the victory.

Chapter 8

A Log Worth Exploring

The warm morning sun spilled over the Monterey Bay, bathing Mia Kingtide's bedroom in golden light. From her desk by the window, she had a perfect view of the bay stretching out before her. The waters sparkled like liquid sapphire, and on the horizon, fishing boats and sailboats bobbed gently in the waves. The sight never failed to make her heart swell with pride and wonder, this was her home, and she loved every part of it.

It was here, in her cozy room overlooking the shimmering expanse of the bay, that Mia often let her imagination run wild. From her window, she could see the water stretching to the horizon, glinting in the sunlight as if inviting her to uncover its secrets. The rhythmic crash of waves against the rocky shoreline below served as a soothing soundtrack to her daydreams. It was in this little sanctuary, surrounded by her collection of seashells, ocean charts, and sketches of marine creatures, that Mia dreamed of the journeys she might one day take, exploring vibrant coral reefs, helping stranded marine animals, or venturing into the mysterious depths where only the bravest divers dared to go.

Today, however, her focus was on the assignment sitting in front of her. The paper, slightly wrinkled from being stuffed into her bag, was a reminder of the task Ms. O'Conner had given them in class the day before.

"Book report due in two weeks," the top of the paper read in bold type. "Choose a book from the list provided. Focus on how it explores the relationship between humans and nature."

Mia leaned back in her chair, tapping a pencil against her notebook. She scanned the reading list for the tenth time. Most of the titles sounded like they were interesting stories of naturalists like John Muir's *My First Summer in the Sierra*, environmentalists like Jack London's *Call of the Wild*, and daring explorers like *Farthest North* by Fridtjof Nansen, but one in particular seemed to call out to her: *The Log from the Sea of Cortez* by John Steinbeck.

Her dad had mentioned the book more than once, often referring to it as one of the most profound and adventurous pieces of writing he'd ever read. "It's not just about science," he'd told her one evening over dinner. "It's about seeing the world differently, understanding how everything is connected. Steinbeck and Ricketts didn't just study life, they lived it, fully and deeply."

Mia's curiosity had been piqued then, and now, with the book on the list, it felt like fate.

She flipped open her laptop and quickly searched for a summary of the book. As she read about Steinbeck and his friend Ed Ricketts' journey to the Sea of Cortez aboard the *Western Flyer*, her excitement grew. The trip wasn't just about collecting specimens; it was about observing life in its rawest, most interconnected form. The idea of blending science, adventure, and philosophy resonated deeply with her.

"This is it," she murmured to herself, circling the title on the reading list. She made a note to ask her dad if they still had a copy of the book.

Her thoughts drifted to what it would have been like to be part of that expedition. She imagined standing on the deck of the *Western Flyer*, the salty breeze in her hair as the ship navigated turquoise waters. In her mind, she could see the tide pools Steinbeck described, teeming with colorful life, each organism playing a vital role in its tiny ecosystem. She wondered what it must have felt like to pull up anchor each day, not knowing what discoveries awaited them beneath the waves.

Mia looked up from the assignment sheet, her gaze shifting back to the bay outside her window. She could see kayaks gliding across the water, seabirds diving for fish, and a sailboat lazily making its way toward the harbor. It was scenes like this that reminded her of why she loved the ocean so much. The thought of exploring it in the same way Steinbeck and Ricketts had filled her with a sense of possibility.

"Maybe one day," she whispered to herself, "I'll have an adventure like that."

As the sun dipped lower in the sky, she bounded down the stairs to find her dad tinkering with something in the garage. Sure enough, there it was: a worn, hardcover copy of *The Log from the Sea of Cortez*, resting on a shelf alongside a few other ocean-themed books.

"You've got good taste, kiddo," Luke said with a grin as she held up the book. "You're gonna love that one. It's a real classic."

"Did you read it when you were my age?" Mia asked, flipping through the pages and admiring the simple, elegant illustrations.

"Not until college," Luke admitted, wiping his hands on a rag. "But it's one of those books that sticks with you. Steinbeck had this way of making you feel like you were right there with him, exploring the tide pools and thinking about life's big questions."

Mia clutched the book tightly. "I think this is the one, Dad. It feels... special."

"It is," Luke said, ruffling her hair. "And hey, maybe one day, we'll take *Pegasus* down to the Sea of Cortez. Who knows? You could write your own log."

Mia loved spending time on *Pegasus*, the family's 34ft CHB aft cabin trawler. It was stored in a marina in the Sacramento Delta for a change of pace from Monterey Bay. Mia loved watching San Francisco Giant's baseball games from the flybridge in McCovey Cove and taking it to the many small towns and cities in the delta.

Mia laughed, but the idea lingered in her mind. The Sea of Cortez, its name alone sounded magical.

As she climbed back up to her room, book in hand, she couldn't help but daydream about what adventures might await her, not just in the pages of Steinbeck's classic, but in the vast, unpredictable ocean she loved so much.

Later that day, Mia perched on the small wooden bench on her deck, her knees drawn up and *The Log from the Sea of Cortez* balanced on her lap. The breeze carried the salty tang of Monterey Bay, and gulls cried overhead as she cracked open the book for the first time. The cover was slightly worn, a testament to how often it had been read. She ran her fingers over it before diving into the pages, Steinbeck's words immediately pulling her into another time and place.

Mia imagined herself aboard the *Western Flyer*, the wooden deck creaking beneath her feet as the ship cut through the turquoise waters of the Sea of Cortez. In her mind, she could see Steinbeck and Ricketts leaning over the side, nets in hand, pulling up buckets of sea life to examine. The way Steinbeck wrote about the tide pools, teeming with creatures both familiar and alien, felt so vivid that Mia could almost hear the faint bubbling of water and the clicking of crab claws.

Her dad stepped out onto the porch, sugar free Red Bull in his hand. "How's it going?" he asked, leaning on the railing.

Mia looked up, her eyes sparkling. "It's amazing," she said, her voice filled with awe. "I love how Steinbeck talks about the ocean like it's alive, like it's its own character. He doesn't just describe the animals; he writes about how everything is connected, like one big web."

Luke chuckled, taking a sip. "That's what makes it so special. It's not just about the science it's about the story of life itself. Ricketts had a way of seeing the world that was ahead of his time, and Steinbeck turned that into something people could feel."

Mia nodded, flipping a page. "It's funny… when Steinbeck talks about pulling up octopuses and crabs and sea cucumbers, I feel like I can relate. Remember when we found that old life raft and freed all those trapped animals? It's kind of the same thing, learning about the creatures, seeing how they live, and figuring out how to help them."

Luke smiled. "I think you and Ricketts would've gotten along. Did you know we can see his old lab from our house? Its right there across the bay beside the Monterey Bay Aquarium."

As she continued reading, Mia found herself drawn to the descriptions of the tide pools, which reminded her of her own adventures at Asilomar Beach in Pacific Grove. She pictured herself crouched over the shimmering pools, her GoPro in hand, marveling at the colorful sea anemones and tiny fish darting between rocks. She remembered how her heart had raced when she first spotted the octopus that gave her the magical shell, and how that moment had changed her life forever.

Mia reached a passage where Steinbeck wrote about the way the crew collected specimens, carefully observing each creature before logging it and preserving it in a jar. She was a little disturbed that they killed what they collected, but she also understood that they didn't have the photography and video tools they have today. It struck a chord with her. "Dad, listen to this," she said, reading aloud. "'It is advisable to look from the tide pool to the stars and then back to the tide pool again.' Isn't that beautiful? It's like he's saying that everything is connected, from the smallest crab to the whole universe."

Luke leaned back against the railing; his gaze fixed on the horizon. "That's exactly it. The more you understand about the little things, the more you understand about the big picture. And vice versa."

Mia's mind wandered to their dives at Mavericks, where she and her dad had explored the underwater rock formations that created the legendary surf break. She thought about how the geology of the sea floor shaped the waves, just as the interconnected ecosystems shaped the life around them. Steinbeck's observations made her realize that she was already living out her own version of the *Sea of Cortez*, every adventure she had on *Pitter Patter* was a chapter in her own logbook of discovery.

As the sun dipped lower in the sky, painting the bay in hues of gold and pink, Mia closed the book and reached for her notebook. Inspired by Steinbeck's writing, she began jotting down ideas for her report.

"*The Log from the Sea of Cortez* is more than just a book about science," she wrote. "It's a story about how humans and nature are part of the same big adventure. Steinbeck and Ricketts didn't just collect specimens, they found meaning in the way all life is connected. It's the same lesson I've learned from the ocean. Whether I'm freeing a trapped shark or helping a harbor seal, it's about understanding the balance and doing my part to protect it."

As she wrote, her excitement for the class presentation grew. She wanted her classmates to see the ocean the way she did not just as a distant, blue expanse, but as a vibrant, living world that needed their care and respect.

Mia glanced at her dad, who was sitting nearby, watching the sunset. "Do you think Steinbeck and Ricketts ever imagined how many people their book would inspire?"

Luke smiled, the fading light softening his features. "Steinbeck was already a famous author when The Log from the Sea of Cortez was published, and Ed Ricketts' work at Pacific Biological Laboratories was changing how people viewed the ocean. He helped shift perspectives from seeing it as something to exploit to recognizing it as an ecosystem that needs care and respect. Sadly, Ricketts passed away just a few years after the first edition came out, but the book gained even more significance after that. I think they'd be proud to see you learning from their lessons and carrying them forward."

Chapter 9

Presentations and Surprises

The 7th grade classroom buzzed with energy as students prepared to present their book reports. Ms. O'Conner moved among the desks, offering encouraging smiles and helping a few nervous students adjust their notes. Mia sat near the middle of the room, her carefully written report tucked neatly into a folder. Beside her, Jessica was flipping through her own notes, excitement written all over her face.

"I can't believe you chose *The Call of the Wild*," Mia whispered. "That book is so intense!"

Jessica grinned, her eyes lighting up. "I know, right? Buck's journey from being a spoiled house dog to surviving in the wild was incredible. The way he connects to his instincts, his true nature, it's like he becomes something more than just a dog."

Mia nodded thoughtfully. "It's amazing how Jack London wrote that. I watched the movie a while ago, I don't think I could ever handle that much snow and ice."

Jessica laughed. "Same! I mean, I can barely deal with the cold here. But the part where Buck finally leads the pack, he's free, in charge, and completely wild, that gave me chills. It's like he was meant to find that life."

Mia tilted her head. "It's kind of like *The Sea of Cortez* in a way, though. I mean, Steinbeck and Ricketts weren't surviving in the wilderness, but they were following their instincts, exploring something unknown and wild in their own way."

Jessica raised an eyebrow. "I guess I never thought of it like that. But you're right, they both have this deep respect for nature, even if the environments are totally different. What was your favorite part of *The Sea of Cortez*?"

Mia smiled. "I loved how Steinbeck described the tide pools, how every creature, no matter how small, had its place and purpose. It's like the ocean has its own kind of wild, but instead of being harsh like the Arctic, it's alive with color and mystery. And unlike Buck, Steinbeck and Ricketts didn't conquer it, they just observed and tried to understand it."

Jessica leaned back, crossing her arms. "That's pretty cool, actually. Maybe Buck's journey and Steinbeck's are both about connecting to something bigger than yourself, whether it's the arctic wilderness or the ocean."

Mia grinned. "Exactly. It's about finding your place in the world and respecting the forces that shape it."

Jessica gave her a playful nudge. "You've got a pretty good way of looking at it, Mia. But I'll stick with dogs over tide pools."

"Fair enough," Mia said, laughing. "I'll take the ocean any day."

At the front of the class, Ms. O'Conner clapped her hands for attention. "Alright, everyone! Let's begin our presentations. Remember, this is about exploring the relationship between humans and nature, so focus on the themes and lessons you discovered in your books."

Jessica was first. She strode confidently to the front of the room, holding a well-worn copy of *The Call of the Wild*.

"This book is about a dog named Buck," she began, her voice steady. "He starts as a pampered pet, but after being taken to the Yukon during the gold rush, he discovers his wild instincts and learns to survive in the harsh wilderness. What really struck me is how Buck's journey mirrors how humans can adapt when we're forced to face challenges. It's a reminder that nature can be both beautiful and brutal."

Jessica went on to describe the vivid landscapes and how Jack London captured the raw power of the wilderness. The class listened intently, and when she finished, there was a burst of applause.

"Great job, Jessica," Ms. O'Conner said warmly.

Next up was Ryan. He adjusted shirt collar nervously as he walked to the front of the room, clutching a thick book about John Muir.

"I chose to read about John Muir because I've been to Yosemite with my family," Ryan began. "Muir's writings about the Sierras are like love letters to the mountains. He didn't just explore them, he wanted to protect them."

Ryan shared quotes from Muir's journals, describing towering waterfalls, ancient sequoias, and the peace he found in the wilderness. "What I learned is that one person can make a huge difference. Muir's passion for nature helped create the national park system, which means those places will be there for future generations."

The class clapped enthusiastically, and Mia gave Ryan a shaka as he returned to his seat.

Finally, it was Mia's turn. She took a deep breath, grabbed her folder, and walked to the front of the room. Her nerves melted away as she looked out at her classmates, many of whom were leaning forward, curious about her choice.

"My book is *The Log from the Sea of Cortez* by John Steinbeck," Mia began, holding up her copy. "It's about a journey Steinbeck took with his friend Ed Ricketts aboard a boat called the *Western Flyer*. They traveled to the Sea of Cortez to study marine life, but the book isn't just about science, it's about how humans and nature are connected."

She described the tide pools teeming with strange creatures, the camaraderie of the crew, and the deep philosophical questions Steinbeck posed about life and the universe. "What stood out to me the most was how they saw the ocean not just as a resource, but as a living, breathing entity. They treated the animals they studied and collected with a bit of awe, and they understood that everything in the ocean is connected, just like everything on land."

Mia went on to share how the book inspired her own adventures and helping at the Marine Mammal

Center. "Steinbeck and Ricketts showed me that we all have a role to play in protecting and participating in nature. It's not just about studying it; it's about making a difference."

When she finished, the room erupted in applause. Even Ms. O'Conner looked impressed. "Wonderful job, Mia. You captured the spirit of the book beautifully."

Mia returned to her seat, her heart racing with pride. As the applause died down, Ms. O'Conner stepped forward with a mysterious smile. "Now, class, I have a special surprise for you. Next week, we'll be taking a field trip to Moss Landing."

There were gasps and murmurs of excitement.

"But that's not all," Ms. O'Conner continued. "We'll be going out on the real *Western Flyer*, the same boat Steinbeck and Ricketts used on their journey. It's been restored, and we've been invited to learn about its history and the marine life of Monterey Bay." Mia's eyes widened, and her hands shot into the air. "Really? The *Western Flyer*?"

"Yes, Mia," Ms. O'Conner said, laughing at her enthusiasm. "I thought it would be the perfect way to bring everything we've learned about humans and nature to life."

As the bell rang and students began to pack up, Mia couldn't contain her excitement. She turned to Jessica and Ryan. "Can you believe it? We're going on the *Western Flyer*! This is going to be amazing."

Jessica grinned. "Looks like your book report is coming to life."

Ryan nodded. "And who knows? Maybe we'll discover something new just like Steinbeck and Ricketts did."

Chapter 10

Aboard the *Western Flyer*

The morning air was crisp and filled with anticipation as Mia and her classmates gathered outside their school. A bright yellow bus idled at the curb, ready to take them on their long-awaited field trip to Moss Landing. Backpacks loaded with notebooks, snacks, and cameras slung over their shoulders, the students chattered excitedly, their voices mingling in a crescendo of excitement.

Mia, standing next to Jessica and Ryan, gripped her notebook tightly, she also had her green waterproof bag with her shell, GoPro and VHF radio that she never left behind. Her mind buzzed with everything she had read about the *Western Flyer*. Today, she would finally step aboard the legendary ship that had inspired so much of her imagination.

"Alright, everyone!" Ms. O'Conner called out, her clipboard in hand. "Let's load up. Find a seat, and we'll be on our way in just a few minutes."

Mia climbed aboard the bus and found a window seat, her heart racing as the wheels began to turn. The drive to Moss Landing was filled with scenic coastal views, with the Pacific Ocean shimmering on one side and rolling farmland stretching out on the other.

As the bus rolled closer to Moss Landing, the iconic twin smokestacks of the Moss Landing Power Plant came into view. Rising high above the coastal landscape, they were a stark reminder of the area's industrial past. For decades, the power plant had been one of the largest natural gas facilities on the California coast, churning out energy and carbon emissions at an extraordinary rate. Burning vast amounts of natural gas to meet the state's energy needs, the plant had contributed to air pollution and climate change.

But in the past decade, Moss Landing had undergone a transformation. Most of the natural gas turbines had been dismantled and the infrastructure had been recycled into one of the largest battery energy storage systems in the world. The massive facility now housed rows upon rows of gleaming, white containers filled with advanced lithium iron phosphate (LiFePO4) batteries. These batteries stored excess energy generated by California's solar farms and wind turbines during the day and fed it back into the grid when the sun wasn't shining, or the wind wasn't blowing. Now, the Moss Landing battery plant was a shining example of how innovation could replace reliance on fossil fuels.

"Did you know," Mia said to Jessica, who was seated beside her, "this used to be one of the biggest carbon emitters on the coast? Now it's helping fight climate change. It's kind of amazing."

Jessica nodded. "I heard they had a lot of problems in the beginning, though. Fires and stuff."

"They did," Mia agreed. "But once they switched to LiFePO4 batteries, those problems basically disappeared. It's kind of like Jessie's boat, a crabber I met in Half Moon Bay, safer and better for the environment. Plus, this place can store so much power from solar and wind. It's way better than burning gas."

As the bus turned off Highway 1, the students caught glimpses of the sprawling battery facility, its clean, futuristic design a stark contrast to the industrial look of the old plant.

When the bus pulled into the small harbor, Mia caught her first glimpse of the *Western Flyer*. It was docked at the end of a pier, its sleek wooden hull restored to its former glory. At 77 feet long and 25 feet wide, the ship wasn't large by modern standards, but its presence was commanding. The freshly polished brass fittings glinted in the sunlight, and its name, *Western Flyer*, was painted boldly on the bow. "Wow," Jessica whispered, leaning toward the window. "It's beautiful."

As they filed off the bus, a man stepped forward to greet them. He was tall, with a calm demeanor that radiated experience. Dressed in a weathered cap and practical jacket, his presence matched the history of the ship he captained.

"Welcome aboard," he said, his voice steady and welcoming. "I'm Paul Tate, the captain of the *Western Flyer*. It's great to have you here."

Another man stepped forward to join him. "And I'm John Gregg, the founder of the *Western Flyer Foundation*. Together, we're continuing the legacy of this incredible vessel."

Paul gestured toward the dock, where the students could see crew members preparing the boat for departure. "Today, you'll learn about the history of this ship and the marine environment we're so lucky to have right here in Monterey Bay. It's going to be an exciting day."

As they walked toward the dock, Mia couldn't help but marvel at the details of the boat. The polished mahogany trim gleamed in the sunlight, and the deck smelled faintly of salt and varnish, a combination that made Mia feel like she was stepping back in time.

Once aboard, Paul led the group to the bow, where he pointed to the horizon. "This boat was originally built in 1937 and famously used by John Steinbeck and Ed Ricketts during their expedition to the Sea of Cortez. Today, it's been fully restored and outfitted with modern engines, capable of cruising at 10 knots."

John added, "It's not just a piece of history. It's a functional research vessel. Below deck, you'll see state-of-the-art labs designed for marine research, from studying plankton to observing deep-sea life."

Mia followed her classmates as they descended below deck. Her eyes widened at the sight of sleek workstations, complete with microscopes, sampling tools, and digital monitors. A remotely operated vehicle (ROV) was secured nearby, its mechanical arms folded neatly.

Paul smiled as he noticed her interest. "That ROV can dive thousands of feet, letting us explore underwater canyons and ecosystems most people never see."

As they moved through the boat, John shared stories of the restoration process. "Every part of this boat was rebuilt with care, from its Douglas Fir planks to its intricate brass fixtures. The goal was to preserve its spirit while equipping it for modern scientific exploration."

Paul nodded. "It's a privilege to captain this ship. Steinbeck and Ricketts viewed the ocean as a source of wonder and discovery. That's what we hope to share with you today."

Back on deck, Paul gathered the students around. "Our journey today will take us to the Monterey Submarine Canyon, one of the deepest underwater canyons in the world. It's a place teeming with life, and I think you'll find it just as inspiring as Steinbeck and Ricketts did."

Mia exchanged a glance with Jessica and Ryan, her heart racing with excitement. This wasn't just a field trip; it was an adventure. As Paul fired up the engines and the *Western Flyer* began to glide away from the dock, Mia leaned against the railing, ready for whatever discoveries the day might bring.

As the Western Flyer glided through the calm waters of the slough, a few familiar faces or flippers appeared in the distance. Mia's heart lifted when she spotted Marlow, the wise sea otter, floating on his back with his signature stone tucked against his belly.

"Mia!" he called, waving a paw.

Beside him, Luna, the playful sea lion, leapt out of the water in a graceful arc, splashing down near the ship's bow. Flip, the energetic harbor seal, popped his head above the surface, barking his excitement.

"You're really doing it!" Luna called. "Exploring the big ocean on that big boat! Don't forget about us little guys!"

Mia leaned over the rail, grinning. "I could never forget you! Thanks for coming to see us off!"

"You're going to find amazing things," Marlow said with a wise smile. "Remember to share them with everyone when you do."

"We'll keep an eye on the harbor while you're gone!" Flip added, spinning playfully.

The trio swam alongside the ship until it passed the edge of the slough, where the waters widened into the expanse of Monterey Bay. As the Western Flyer picked up speed, Marlow, Luna, and Flip waved their final goodbyes before vanishing beneath the waves.

The Western Flyer's captain, Paul Tate, expertly adjusted the ship's course, heading toward the Monterey Submarine Canyon, a colossal underwater chasm that stretched deeper than the Grand Canyon itself. The atmosphere on the ship buzzed with excitement as students and researchers gathered along the railings and peered out over the open water. The canyon was a renowned hotspot of marine biodiversity, where powerful ocean currents collided and churned nutrients to the surface, creating an irresistible buffet for sea life.

"Keep your eyes peeled, everyone," Captain Tate announced, his voice carrying over the hum of the engines. "This area is famous for surprises."

The students leaned over the rails, scanning the horizon eagerly. The sunlight sparkled on the water like scattered diamonds, and the ocean seemed calm, almost deceptively so. But Mia knew better. Beneath the surface lay a world teeming with life, and it wasn't long before the first sign of that life appeared.

In the distance, a massive dark shape broke the surface, a plume of mist rising high into the air. "It's a humpback!" someone shouted, and the group rushed to get a better view.

More whales appeared, their sleek backs arching gracefully above the water before vanishing again in smooth dives. Each exhalation sent a spray of water into the air, the sound of their breath distinct and powerful. Mia gripped the rail tightly, her heart pounding with excitement. She had seen humpbacks from her kayak before, but there was something extraordinary about witnessing them from this historic ship.

Suddenly, one of the whales breached. The massive creature soared out of the water, twisting in midair before crashing back down with a thunderous splash. Gasps and cheers erupted from the group as water sprayed high into the air, droplets catching the sunlight in a fleeting rainbow.

Ryan, leaned over the railing beside her, his camera clicking rapidly. "That was incredible," he murmured, his eyes wide with awe. "Did you see the size of that splash?"

Mia nodded, unable to tear her eyes away. "It's like they're putting on a show just for us."

The activity on the water intensified as the humpbacks began lunge feeding. The group watched in stunned silence as the whales worked together, surging up through the surface with their mouths wide open. The water boiled with activity as the humpbacks devoured schools of sardines, their massive bodies twisting and turning with precision.

Above the scene, seabirds swarmed, their sharp cries filling the air as they dove fearlessly into the chaos to snatch up whatever the whales missed. Pelicans glided low over the water, their long beaks snapping up fish with practiced ease, while gulls circled overhead, opportunistically diving after every splash.

One particularly bold pelican landed on the water just feet from one of the humpbacks, bobbing precariously as the whale's tail fluke emerged and slapped the surface in a powerful dive. Mia held her breath, watching the delicate balance of nature play out before her eyes.

"Look over there!" Jessica called, pointing excitedly. A smaller humpback calf surfaced near its mother, mimicking her movements. The calf swam beside the larger whale, seemingly trying to copy the lunge-feeding behavior, though it was clearly less practiced.

"They're teaching the next generation," Captain Tate said, his voice filled with admiration. "This is how they pass on survival skills."

Mia's mind raced, thinking of all the ways marine life was interconnected. The humpbacks, the sardines, the seals, the sea lions, and the birds, all part of a delicate balance that relied on the health of the canyon and the nutrient-rich waters it provided.

She glanced at the others, their faces glowing with excitement and awe. "This is what it's all about," she thought, feeling a deep sense of purpose. "Showing people how amazing and important the ocean is."

The whales continued their feeding for several minutes before gradually moving off toward deeper waters. The Western Flyer's engines hummed softly as Captain Tate slowed the vessel to give the majestic creatures plenty of space. Mia watched them disappear into the distance, their spouts fading against the horizon.

"That," Ryan said, lowering his camera and shaking his head, "was something I'll never forget."

Mia nodded, her heart still racing. "Me neither," she said, her voice barely above a whisper.

Once the humpbacks had moved on, their magnificent tails disappearing into the horizon, the deck of the Western Flyer hummed with activity. The research team prepared to deploy the ROV (remotely operated vehicle), its bright orange frame glinting under the sunlight as it was carefully lowered into the water. Mia leaned over the rail, watching the ROV disappear beneath the surface, trailing its cable behind it.

The Western Flyer's lab was alive with excitement as the ROV continued its descent, but Mia couldn't tear her eyes away from the screen. She sat beside Ryan and Jessica, her two closest friends, both equally enthralled by the underwater world unfolding before them.

"Look at that!" Jessica whispered, pointing to a brightly lit translucent fish darting past the camera. "It's like a real-life alien planet."

"Yeah, but better," Ryan added, his tone laced with awe. "No green screen, no computer graphics, just nature being awesome.”

Mia grinned, their enthusiasm matching her own. “This is why I love the ocean. You never know what you’re going to find.”

As the ROV approached the 700-foot mark, the lights illuminated the canyon’s rocky terrain, revealing a breathtaking underwater landscape. Towering rock formations, sculpted by millennia of ocean currents, jutted skyward. Their surfaces were covered in vibrant deep-water hydrocorals, its fiery orange and red hues glowing under the ROV’s lights. Strange fish with translucent bodies glided silently through the water, their forms ghostly and elegant.

“Whoa,” Jessica breathed, leaning closer to the monitor. “That’s insane. Look at all that coral.”

“Hydrocoral,” Mia corrected gently. “It’s not a true coral like the kind that forms reefs. It’s a colonial organism, but it’s just as important. It provides shelter for so many creatures.”

“And check out those crabs!” Ryan pointed to the screen, where a spindly-legged crab clung to the rocks, picking at the coral with its tiny pincers. “They’re like underwater acrobats.”

Then, something unusual caught their attention. A small, free-swimming creature drifted into view, its translucent body shimmering under the lights. The ROV operator zoomed in, and the lab filled with murmurs of curiosity.

Mia’s heart leaped. “It’s a nudibranch!” she exclaimed, her voice rising with excitement.

The tiny sea slug was unlike anything Mia had ever seen. Its body shimmered with iridescent shades of blue and green, and along its back were intricate frilled appendages that waved like ribbons in the water. It moved with slow, undulating motions, its delicate form floating effortlessly.

"Whoa, that's gorgeous," Ryan said, his jaw dropping. "What even is it?"

"Nudibranchs are sea slugs," Mia explained, her voice brimming with passion. "But they're so much more than that. They're some of the most colorful and diverse creatures in the ocean. They recycle toxins from their prey to defend themselves, and some even photosynthesize using algae they eat."

Jessica's eyes widened. "Wait, they can photosynthesize? That's wild."

"It's rare, but yeah," Mia replied. "And this one's capable of free-swimming, which is even more amazing. Most nudibranchs live on the seafloor."

The ROV's camera followed the nudibranch as it swam near a hydrocoral branch, its frilled appendages fluttering like tiny wings. The researchers in the lab were buzzing with excitement.

"This might be a new species," one of the researchers said, jotting down notes. "We'll need to analyze the footage and collect environmental samples."

Mia leaned toward the screen, her heart swelling with wonder. "It's so beautiful. And so fragile. I wonder how many more creatures like this are out there, waiting to be discovered."

Jessica nudged her playfully. "Maybe you'll be the one to find them all, Captain Kingtide."

Ryan grinned. "Yeah, you're practically a marine superhero already."

Mia laughed, but her thoughts lingered on the tiny creature. She felt a deep sense of responsibility to protect the ocean and its secrets. As the ROV continued its exploration, she resolved to share what she'd seen and learned with as many people as possible.

The nudibranch drifted out of view, leaving the group with a sense of awe and a renewed appreciation for the wonders of the deep. Mia turned to Jessica and Ryan, her eyes shining. "We have to tell everyone about this. People need to know how incredible the ocean is."

Jessica nodded. "And how important it is to protect it."

Ryan fist-bumped Mia. "You're right. Let's make sure this little guy gets the spotlight it deserves."

The students from Mia's class stood in small groups, still buzzing with excitement from their unforgettable day. Mia lingered at the railing of the *Western Flyer*, scanning the docks until she spotted her dad, Luke, standing aboard *Pitter Patter*. The bright red hull of their trusty cruiser gleamed in the afternoon sun, and Luke waved enthusiastically.

Captain Paul Tate brought the *Western Flyer* smoothly alongside the dock, and Mia joined her classmates in giving him a round of applause. "Thank you, Captain Tate!" she called, her voice carrying over the water.

He tipped his cap with a warm smile. "Glad you all could be part of the adventure."

As the students disembarked and began boarding their bus back to Monterey, Mia walked down the dock toward her dad. He stood beside the *Western Flyer*, leaning on the railing and chatting animatedly with Captain Tate.

"This beauty is a marvel," Luke said, gesturing to the *Western Flyer*. "The restoration, the labs, everything is perfect. She's more than a ship; she's a legacy."

Captain Tate nodded. "That's exactly what we hoped for. Every time we take her out, it feels like honoring Steinbeck and Ricketts. You're welcome to visit the Flyer anytime."

Mia smiled as she reached them. "Hey, Dad! Captain Tate's been showing us the coolest stuff all day."

"I can tell," Luke said, ruffling her hair. He turned back to Tate. "Thanks for giving them such an incredible experience. I've been following the Flyer's story for years, it's inspiring to see her back in action."

After a few more minutes of enthusiastic conversation, Luke shook Captain Tate's hand. "Thanks again. We'll get out of your way. Mia and I are heading back to Monterey on *Pitter Patter*."

"Safe travels," Tate replied. "And good luck with whatever adventure comes next."

Once they were aboard *Pitter Patter* and clear of the docks, Luke throttled up, guiding the boat into the channel that led back to the open ocean. The twin smokestacks of Moss Landing Power Plant shrank in the distance as the cruiser hummed steadily over the waves.

Mia settled into her usual seat beside the helm, her mind still swirling with thoughts of the day. The humpback whales, the incredible ROV footage, the new nudibranch all of it felt like a dream.

Luke glanced over at her. "So, Miss Kingtide, what was the highlight for you?"

"Everything," Mia said, grinning. "But I think discovering that new nudibranch was the best. It made me feel like I was part of something bigger, you know? Like the ocean still has so many secrets waiting to be found."

Luke smiled knowingly. "You sound just like Ricketts in *The Log from the Sea of Cortez*. I bet he'd be proud of you."

Mia's grin widened, but before she could respond, Luke's tone grew more serious. "Speaking of adventures, I've got something I've been planning to talk to you about."

"What's up?" Mia asked, sitting up straighter.

Luke leaned back in the captain's chair, his hands steady on the wheel. "I've been thinking about our summer. It's been a while since we've taken *Pegasus* out for a long trip. What do you say we outfit her and head south, really south, to the Sea of Cortez?"

Mia's eyes went wide. "Wait, are you serious? The Sea of Cortez?"

"Completely serious," Luke said, his grin matching her excitement. "I've been saving up for this. Eight weeks, a full loop from Monterey to the Sea of Cortez and back. We'll explore the same waters Steinbeck and Ricketts wrote about."

Mia practically jumped out of her seat. "Yes! Absolutely yes! That's the best idea ever!"

Luke laughed. "I figured you'd be on board. Now we just need to figure out who else to bring. We'll need a good crew, people who can handle long days at sea, enjoy exploring, and don't mind helping out."

Mia thought for a moment, her excitement shifting into contemplation. "Maybe Jessica or Ryan? They've been great partners on all our school trips. And they love the ocean as much as I do, but they might be a bit young and probably wouldn't want to give up their whole summer."

Luke nodded thoughtfully, adjusting the throttle slightly. "They'd definitely bring good energy, but yeah, they might not be ready for a trip like this. Anyone else come to mind?"

Mia tapped her chin, her eyes lighting up. "What about Grandpa Kingtide? He knows everything about diesel engines, electrical systems, and all the mechanicals on *Pegasus*. Plus, he loves the ocean as much as you do, and I bet he'd have amazing stories and skills to share."

Luke raised an eyebrow, the corners of his mouth curling into a smile. "That's not a bad idea, Mia. My dad's been tinkering with boats his whole life, and he'd be a huge help. But you know how he is, he loves his home in Canada and Grandma would miss him while he is gone. It might take some convincing to get him to leave for eight weeks."

"We could call him tonight!" Mia suggested eagerly. "If anyone could teach us how to really handle *Pegasus* for a long trip, it's Grandpa and maybe Grandma could come visit us at some point in the trip."

Luke chuckled. "Alright, we'll call him. But if he says yes, you know we'll have to stock a lot of coffee for him. He'll need it to survive without his workshop."

Mia laughed at the thought. "Deal. It'll be worth it."

Luke leaned back in his chair, gazing out at the horizon as *Pitter Patter* cruised steadily toward Monterey harbor. "This trip is going to be amazing, but there's a lot to do before we're ready. *Pegasus* will need some serious upgrades."

Mia's eyes sparkled with curiosity. "Like what?"

"Well," Luke began, "first, we need to swap out her current batteries for LiFePO4 ones. They're safer, more reliable, and perfect for long trips like this. We'll also install more solar panels to help power the electronics and keep the batteries charged when we're anchored or underway. A compressor for scuba tanks is another must-have, there'll be plenty of diving opportunities in the Sea of Cortez, and we don't want to rely on finding dive shops."

"That sounds like a lot of work," Mia said, though her voice was filled with excitement. "Do you think we can get it all done before June?"

"We will, I have friends at the boat yard that can make it happen" Luke replied, his tone determined. "We've got a few months, and we'll start as soon as we're back. Between upgrading the electrical systems, adding a watermaker, and making sure the engines are in top shape, we'll have our hands full. But with a bit of help maybe from Grandpa it's doable."

Mia leaned back against the bench, her mind spinning with possibilities. "We'll need to plan everything, fuel stops, provisions, dive sites, even the weather patterns. It's going to be so much fun!"

Luke smiled at her enthusiasm. "Exactly. It'll be a family project and a family adventure. And by the time we're sailing down the Baja coast, everything will be worth it."

As the restaurants on old Fisherman's wharf of Monterey came into view, Mia felt a surge of excitement. Retracing Steinbeck and Ricketts' journey was no longer just a daydream. With her dad's guidance, *Pegasus* would become their vessel of discovery, and the Sea of Cortez awaited a living, breathing ocean full of mysteries, challenges, and unforgettable moments.

Watch for the next
Mia Kingtide
adventure coming soon!

Learn more and experience
Mia Kingtide's world at:
http://www.pitterpatterdiving.com

You Can Be an Ocean Hero!

Just like Mia Kingtide, you have the power to help the ocean! Every little action counts—whether it's picking up trash on the beach, using less plastic, or learning about the amazing animals that call the ocean home. By protecting the ocean, you're helping sea turtles, dolphins, whales, and even tiny plankton that make the world a better place for everyone. Remember, when we take care of the ocean, it takes care of us. So, grab your friends and family, and let's work together to keep our seas sparkling clean and full of life!

Partnering with or supporting these organizations can help amplify your efforts to protect marine ecosystems.

USA-Based Organizations

Monterey Bay Aquarium Research Institute (MBARI)
Marine research, ocean technology, and conservation.
Get Involved: Education programs, internships, volunteer opportunities.
www.mbari.org

MBARI has a fantastic Open House in July that should not be missed!

Giant Giant Kelp Restoration Project (G2KR)
Dedicated to protecting and actively restoring
California's kelp forest
Get Involved: Urchin Culling, educational
programs, grassroots activism.
g2kr.com

The Sunflower Star Laboratory
Researching and developing sustainable conservation
aquaculture methods for sunflower star conservation
and reintroduction.
Get Involved: Donate or Volunteer to help new
Sunflower Stars return to the bay.
sunflowerstarlab.org

Ocean Conservancy
Fighting for trash-free seas, protecting Arctic and
coastal ecosystems.
Get Involved: International Coastal Cleanup, policy
advocacy, donations.
www.oceanconservancy.org

Surfrider Foundation
Clean beaches, ocean protection, and climate action.
Get Involved: Beach cleanups, grassroots activism,
membership.
www.surfrider.org

NOAA Marine Debris Program
Reducing marine debris through research, removal,
and prevention.
Get Involved: Educational resources, cleanup
initiatives, grants.
marinedebris.noaa.gov

Pacific Marine Mammal Center

Rescuing and rehabilitating marine mammals in California.

Get Involved: Donations, internships, volunteer opportunities.

www.pacificmmc.org

Marine Conservation Institute

Protecting marine ecosystems through research and advocacy.

Get Involved: Support marine protected areas (MPAs), advocacy campaigns.

marine-conservation.org

Global Organizations

The Ocean Cleanup

Removing plastic pollution from the ocean and preventing riverborne trash.

Get Involved: Donations, educational resources, technology development.

www.theoceancleanup.com

Plastic Oceans International

Addressing plastic pollution through education, science, and advocacy.

Get Involved: Educational campaigns, events, donations.

plasticoceans.org

World Wildlife Fund (WWF) – Oceans Program
Conserving marine species, protecting ecosystems, and reducing threats to oceans.
Get Involved: Advocacy, educational programs, donations.
www.worldwildlife.org

Mission Blue
Creating and protecting "Hope Spots"—areas critical to the health of the ocean.
Get Involved: Hope Spot nominations, advocacy, support.
mission-blue.org

PADI AWARE Foundation
Marine conservation through diving education and citizen science.
Get Involved: Dive Against Debris programs, marine species protection.
www.padi.com/aware

International Union for Conservation of Nature (IUCN) – Marine and Polar Programme
Supporting global efforts to protect marine biodiversity.
Get Involved: Policy development, conservation projects, scientific studies.
www.iucn.org

UN Environment Programme (UNEP) – Clean Seas Campaign

Reducing marine litter and plastic pollution globally.
Get Involved: Advocacy campaigns, partnerships, educational initiatives.
www.cleanseas.org

Ocean Wise

Promoting sustainable seafood, reducing ocean pollution, and marine research.
Get Involved: Education programs, research, sustainable seafood initiatives.
ocean.org

Academic and Research Institutions

Woods Hole Oceanographic Institution
Ocean science and engineering.
www.whoi.edu

Scripps Institution of Oceanography (USA)
Marine biology, climate science, and oceanography.
scripps.ucsd.edu

Oceanographic Museum of Monaco
Marine research and public education.
www.oceano.org

Schmidt Ocean Institute
Advancing oceanographic research through technology and exploration.
schmidtocean.org

How to Get Involved

Volunteer: Join local beach cleanups, citizen science projects, or educational programs.

Advocate: Support policies that protect marine environments.

Donate: Contribute to organizations focused on ocean conservation.
Educate: Share resources and knowledge about ocean conservation with your community.

Collaborate: Partner with schools, nonprofits, and research institutions to raise awareness and fund projects.

Each of these organizations plays a unique role in safeguarding our oceans, and your participation can make a big difference!

Pitter Patter
26ft Shamrock 260 Express

Pegasus
CHB Aft Cabin Trawler

**Mia Kingtide :
Journey to the Sea of Cortez
is Coming Soon
Read the first chapter!**

Chapter 1

Journey to Monterey

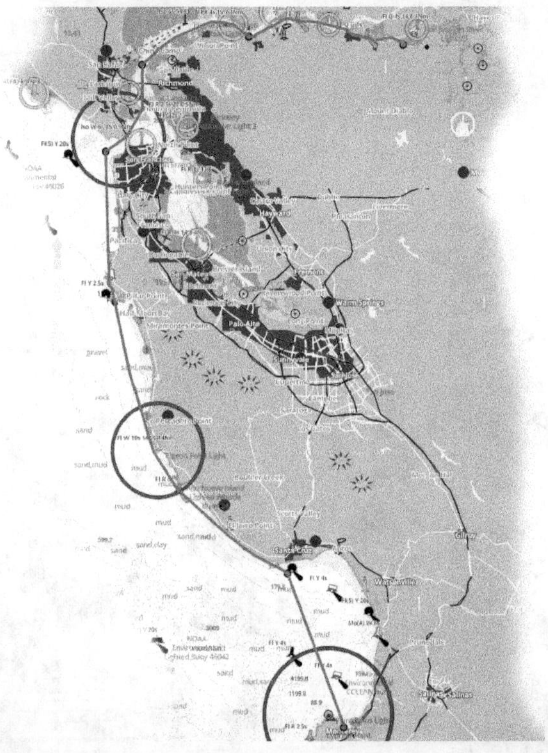

The early morning sun cast a soft glow on the Sacramento Delta, glinting off the water as Pegasus, the 34-foot CHB Trawler, gently rocked at her mooring. Mia Kingtide stood on the deck, her blonde hair pulled back into a braid, as she took in the scene. The newly polished teak railings gleamed, and the gentle hum of the engine beneath her feet sent a thrill of excitement through her.

Today marked the beginning of a new adventure, a journey that would take them from the Delta, down the California coast, and ultimately to the Sea of Cortez.

"Mia, grab the fenders, would you?" her dad, Luke, called from the flybridge. He was adjusting the throttle, his Mariners cap tipped low over his forehead. His voice was calm, but there was an edge of excitement in it, too.

Built in 1977 in Taiwan, Pegasus was a testament to the craftsmanship of the era. At 34 feet long and with a width or beam of 13 feet, she was compact yet surprisingly spacious, designed to be a practical and economical cruising vessel. These trawlers were popular for their affordability, seaworthiness, and efficient operation, and Pegasus was no exception.

The boat was divided into three key sections. At the bow was the V-berth, which had become Mia's personal sanctuary. It featured its own small bathroom with a marine toilet and sink, giving her a cozy space to call her own during long voyages. The aft cabin, a bit more spacious, housed a double bed on one side and a single on the other, with another bathroom tucked away for convenience. This was where her dad, Luke Kingtide and Grandpa Jim Kingtide would stay, surrounded by decades of experience and stories from the sea.

The center saloon served as the heart of the boat. With a small but efficient galley that included a sink, a refrigerator, an induction hot plate and a microwave, it was where meals were prepared and conversations flowed. The saloon also had an interior helm station, giving a place to steer the boat during rough weather or long nights. Above, the flybridge offered another helm, providing a panoramic view for navigating and a favorite spot for relaxing in calm seas.

Pegasus was equipped for versatility. A mast held the radar, ensuring they could safely traverse foggy or busy waters, and a windlass at the bow managed the heavy anchor that would keep them securely moored in the bays and coves they planned to explore. At the stern, the swim platform provided easy access to the water, perfect for Mia's diving and swimming excursions. Powered by a reliable six-cylinder Perkins diesel engine, Pegasus burned only two gallons of diesel an hour, making her incredibly efficient. With two 110-gallon fuel tanks, she had a 800+ mile range perfect for extended voyages, like the one they were planning to the Sea of Cortez. She also carried 50 gallons of freshwater and 37 gallons of waste storage, essentials for a boat designed for living aboard.

Mia nodded and quickly hauled in the fenders, her hands working with practiced ease. "All clear, Dad!" she called, securing the last line.

Her grandfather, Jim Kingtide, appeared from below deck, a steaming mug of coffee in hand. At seventy-five, his rugged face bore the weathered lines of a life spent working and adventuring on the water. A retired industrial maintenance expert from Canada, he had flown down to join them on their journey and lend his expertise in preparing Pegasus for the two-month voyage ahead.

"Beautiful morning for a run," Jim said, settling into the saloon. He leaned back, the faint aroma of coffee mixing with the salty morning air. "But it's going to be a long one. How's the old girl running?"

Luke gave him a thumbs-up from the helm. "Purring like a kitten, Dad. That new fuel filter you installed made a world of difference."

Jim chuckled, taking a sip of his coffee. "Good. We'll need her running smooth if we're heading all the way down to the Sea of Cortez. By the way, we should talk about solar panels and upgrading the batteries to Lithium Iron Phosphate. Those old lead-acid ones aren't going to cut it for what you're planning."

Luke nodded in agreement. "Absolutely. We'll need solar for the fridge, heat pump, navigation systems, and to run the compressor for scuba tanks. And LFP batteries are safer and more reliable, worth every penny, especially now they are even cheaper, safer and lighter than the lead acid ones."

As Pegasus eased out of the Sacramento Delta, the morning sun lit up the waterways, casting a golden glow on the landscape. They moved through the San Francisco Bay. The day was calm, the water stretching out before them like an invitation to adventure.

Mia stood on the fly bridge, her heart swelling as the Pacific Ocean came into view through the Golden Gate. Her excitement was tempered only by her growing list of ideas for upgrading Pegasus. The boat wasn't just a means of transportation; it was about to become their home for the next two months. She turned to her dad and grandpa, both deep in conversation about diesel engines and navigation systems, and smiled. This wasn't just a family trip, it was the start of something extraordinary.

Mia stood at the bow, taking in the view as sailboats, giant container ships and fast ferrys dotted the water around them.

"Angel Island's got some history," Jim said, joining her at the bow. "It was the Ellis Island of the West Coast, immigrants, mostly from Asia, came through here. But it was also a military base for years."

"Do people still live there?" Mia asked, her curiosity piqued.

"Not anymore," Jim replied. "But it's a state park now. Great spot for hiking and picnicking."

The Golden Gate Bridge loomed ahead, its iconic red-orange towers disappearing into the morning mist. Mia couldn't help but feel a flutter of excitement as Pegasus passed beneath it.

"Dad, look at that view!" Mia called, snapping a picture with her GoPro.

Luke smiled from the helm. "Pretty amazing, huh? This never gets old."

As they cleared the bridge and entered open water, the Pacific stretched out before them, vast and endless. Pegasus settled into her cruising speed of seven knots, her engine thrumming steadily. The waves were calm, and the breeze carried the salty tang of the ocean.

Their first landmark was Half Moon Bay, a picturesque harbor nestled against the coast. They didn't stop but waved at a few fishing boats heading out for the day. Mia remembered their time there with the crabbers and smiled, feeling a connection to the small community.

The day wore on as they cruised past Año Nuevo, famous for its elephant seal rookery. Mia kept a lookout, hoping to spot one of the massive creatures basking on the beach, but they were too far offshore. Jim took over the helm for a while, letting Luke and Mia stretch their legs on deck.

As the sun dipped lower on the horizon, the coastline began to change. The rugged cliffs and golden beaches of Monterey Bay came into view, their beauty amplified by the soft evening light. They were almost home.

It was Memorial Day weekend, and celebrations dotted the coastline. From Santa Cruz to Monterey, fireworks lit up the night sky, their bright colors reflecting off the water. Pegasus cruised steadily along, her wake glowing in the light of the explosions.

"Look at that!" Mia exclaimed, pointing to a particularly impressive display. "It's like the whole coast is celebrating with us."

Jim chuckled. "Or welcoming us back to Monterey."

By the time they reached Monterey Harbor, it was well past midnight. Luke guided Pegasus into the boat yard dock with the precision of a seasoned captain, and the family worked together to tie her up securely.

As Mia stepped onto the dock, she felt a mix of exhaustion and exhilaration. The journey had been long, but it was only the beginning. The Sea of Cortez awaited, and with her dad and grandfather by her side, she knew it would be an adventure of a lifetime.

Get your copy of

**Mia Kingtide :
Journey to the Sea of Cortez**

to read the rest of the story

**Available at
http://pitterpatterdiving.com**

About the Author

Luke Kilpatrick, based in Sand City along California's stunning Pacific Coast, is a passionate storyteller and explorer of all things California. His books delve into the beauty, culture, and spirit of the coastal regions and the Golden State at large. An avid scuba diver, photographer, surfer, and  boater, Luke brings his deep connection to the ocean and outdoors to life in his writing and his puzzle books.

With a career that began in graphic design and software development, Luke transitioned to developer marketing and relations, where he's excelled for over 15 years. When he's not crafting stories or navigating the tech world, he manages The Ocean View at Monterey Bay, a charming vacation rental where guests are invited to take his books home as a memento of their stay. Luke's love for California shines through in his work, blending his talents and passions to celebrate the state's unparalleled landscapes and lifestyle.

Connect with Luke:

Website: www.pitterpatterdiving.com

Twitter: @lkilpatrick

Facebook: facebook.com/lukekilpatrick

TikTok: PitterPatterDiving

www.ingramcontent.com/pod-product-compliance
Lightning Source LLC
Chambersburg PA
CBHW071533100726
47908CB00004B/1381